The Bexley Affair

A Harry Potts Novel

Dick Redfern

PublishAmerica
Baltimore

ISBN: 1-4241-7870-3
PUBLISHED BY PUBLISHAMERICA, LLLP
www.publishamerica.com
Baltimore

Printed in the United States of America

For Esther, one of
our most-improved
golfers.
    Best Regards,

        Dick Redfern

CHAPTER ONE

My housekeeper Mrs. Hoskins had left a message; a phone number requiring a call back.

Arriving home as I had, from a successful and an enjoyable night on the dartboard and being suitably mellowed by the brown-ales provided by the losers, I noted the unfamiliar number; which almost invariably meant clients—and decided it could wait until later. After all who is likely to hire an investigator—who can't find a syllable with his tongue?

The profession that chose me is perhaps one of "finder" rather than investigator. A finder of missing odds and sods—that's me. Some of the items have been odd, and some of the people, proper sods. However, the recovery rate of both has had a stimulating effect on my personal worth. I am not by nature, a greedy person; on the other hand I do like the nicer things in life, so incoming funds in large dollops aren't to be sniffed at. To sum it up, the finding business is not a bad paying lark.

There is no doubt, that the "Finchley Caper," as the newspaper lads dubbed it, together with my much publicised role in it a couple of years ago, led me into this unusual career. A chap would have to be a fool, not to take advantage of all that exposure provided by Fleet Street. We are, I suppose, all fools in one way or another; but turning my back on the opportunity to make a profit is not a weakness of mine.

When the letters began to cascade through my letterbox, offering me fat fees to find something or someone, it all became irresistible. I just drifted along with the flow and by careful selection of the right currents, err—cases, I've been fairly successful. Mind you, when clients are lining up to pay money for a chap's services—there is not much sense in picking the tough assignments, right?

So, with the Finchley thing as a springboard, you could say I dropped into the finding game. An uncouth person might also suggest that it's been better, than dropping into some things which spring to mind—they wouldn't get much of an argument from me.

However, to get back to the message and the phone number requiring a call back: I judged it prudent to defer returning the call until the morning. A good night of sleep usually works wonders with the agility of my tongue.

So then, when my housekeeper Mrs. Hoskins maliciously disturbed me, I knew morning had arrived, and also knew, that I was nowhere near ready for it. Her voice penetrated the fog of my slumber like a foghorn gone berserk.

I held up a finger, in a plea for silence. It didn't work.

"Mr. Potts, time to wake up," shrieked Mrs. H; to officially open the day, "Did you call that number?" she screamed, without a hint of pity for my fragile condition. "Said she was Lady Bexley's secretary, and you was to call. Grand company you're keeping Mr. Potts."

Thankfully, she stopped her hysterics while she relocated the rubbish on my bedside table to make room for my morning cup of tea.

I should explain that Mrs. H, bless her heart, looks after my cottage, and me, when I'm "in residence" as she puts it. She lives a short walk along the road, and is usually here before I get up, waking me in due course with the cup of tea routine. Mrs. H is a real gem; although a trifle narrow minded. I have to watch my conduct about the house. She is not slow to set me straight if I don't draw the line according to her standards. Which I hasten to add, are not severe enough for me to run the risk of jeopardising the care she takes of my creature comforts. Anyway, I'm fond of her.

"Come along Mr. Potts drink it while it's hot."

I knew her voice would persist longer than I could resist, so I sat up in a show of surrender, adding a sickly smile to show that I could lose with good grace. It did the trick; I watched the bow of her retreating apron bob its way out of the room.

In due course; recovery more or less complete, I phoned the Bexley number and agreed to present my person that afternoon. The location of the Bexley place was less than an hour drive from my place, which put us in the same county of Kent...perhaps the prettiest county in England, and thus known as the "garden of England" with just cause.

* * * *

I had invested some time this morning in researching Sir Aubrey and Lady Bexley. Sir Aubrey (give the man a cigar) had passed his credit check with colours flying. If he had the need, together with a fair degree of desire, he'd be able to afford me! My fee structure is amazingly flexible; which means that I stretch it as far as I can. "Whatever the traffic will bear" has a nice ring to it.

Directions had been given me on my brief phone call, on how best to get to the Bexley residence. Weald Hall, Dunkinge, Kent, was the simple address. I mentally placed a Hall as half a step less than a Castle, so I was geared for something on the grand scale...I got that right! As it hove into view, my fee started to flex its muscle; it was happy with what it saw.

Some place! It may have been in the same county as mine, which was about all they had in "common"...a word that should be whispered in the presence of such magnificence.

As I swung off the road, and entered through the opened heavy wrought iron gates, a driveway of honey coloured immaculately groomed gravel beckoned me towards the Hall. My passing disturbed the gravel; prompting it to herald my approach with a muted crunching chorus. Marble statues, their graceful postures cast in time, did their best to intimidate me. I wasn't, so another couple of statues wearing old clothes, probably gardeners, touched their caps as I passed them by…a nice touch!

Altogether, the setting exuded an aura of elegance and wealth.

As I parked my Bentley at the foot of the steps, and climbed up to the entrance, I looked back down and thought how well the old girl looked in that setting.

An elderly gentleman, summoned by the peal of bells activated by my finger on the bell push, admitted me, after I replied "Mr. Potts" to the query of his raised eyebrows.

"If you will follow me sir," he suggested, "Lady Bexley is expecting you."

I played follow-the-leader with him. He had to be fitter than he looked—it was a long walk.

We traversed floors of flagstone, marble tile, polished oak, and an expensive looking acreage of carpets. My shoes had seldom had it so good.

At journey's end I was ushered into a glassed-in, plant strewn patio.

Seated with her legs curled up under her on a brightly cushioned white wicker bench, was a dark-haired woman of about thirty-five, who started to uncoil and rise as my guide announced, "Mr. Potts, my Lady."

Not an impressive announcement, given the opulent surroundings. Not that I wish to put too much blame on the old lad, he probably did as well as could be expected with the material he had to work with. Now, "Lord Potts," delivered in the same manner would have given his line much more weight…wouldn't have done my ego any harm either!

My attention swivelled back to the Lady who was putting on quite a show as she demonstrated the art of uncoiling, from the wink of the cleavage to the wriggle of her hips, as she ran a caressing hand over their contours in the act of smoothing her dress. The Lady had, without any argument, an attractive composition of moving parts, and she knew how to use them.

Interesting eyes too which she allowed me ample time to explore. Eyes of brown; deep eyes, that were busy taking stock of me. My eyes were busy making eyes at hers, and both seemed satisfied with the effort.

However, the only reaction she showed was the hint of a social smile, and, "Thank you for coming Mr. Potts. I do appreciate your making it so promptly."

I thought there was a hint of sarcasm there, so I replied politely that the pleasure was all mine and wished I could have come sooner.

We both recited a few more platitudes, during which time she had rearranged herself back on the bench and I had suggested she call me Harry.

Demonstrating that that was OK, she said. "I have been trying to decide, Harry, whether you are American. Your accent rather intrigues me."

"Does it," I replied as I sat down in the chair my guide had proffered before he vanished. "Brief explanation," I went on. "I was born in England, right here in Kent. In fact, as I was born south of the Medway I rate as a Man of Kent. Then I spent my younger years in North America, divided fairly evenly between the States and Canada, so some of that accent rubbed off on me. Then, when war broke out I came back to England and joined the RAF, which had its own slang, some of which probably stuck. So there you have it, I'm at home on both sides of the Atlantic. In England, I often get the question you just asked. In Canada, or the States, I'm most likely to get the comment, "Say, you're English." I'm semiliterate in both languages…boot or trunk, lift or elevator, guy or bloke…take your pick. I've stopped trying to translate."

"You were a pilot then during the war?" asked Lady Bexley.

"No, I was a dispatch rider," I replied.

"Oh really, you mean you delivered notes and things?" she sounded disappointed.

"That about sums it up," I agreed. "But perhaps it's time we discussed your problem Lady Bexley."

"I'll come to that in just a moment." she murmured, then went on, "Do you know Vancouver, in British Columbia?"

"Not well, but I know where it is"

"That's good…" Her voice faltered and the comment sat there. She took a deep breath, which drew my attention in a hurry back to the cleavage. Then she apparently made up her mind about something. "Mr. Potts…err Harry, "(which dragged my interest reluctantly back to business) "I did tell you," she went on, "when we spoke on the telephone; who suggested that I contact you. Well he of course, assured me of your integrity. Even so, I must have your word, before I dare discuss the…situation; that you will treat the matter as absolutely confidential."

The client was beginning to show emotion. As she stopped talking, her lips were trembling. Which was enough for me to begin to ask myself—what kind of situation is she going to toss at me?

If I was going to find out, without the interruption of tears, I thought I should offer some assurance. This was one Lady who wasn't going to keep a stiff upper lip much longer.

"Lady Bexley," I said in a suitably compassionate tone. "Things are seldom as black as they appear. I am here to help you…so let me. Whatever you tell me, stops right here. Nobody drags a word out of Harry Potts, so just tell me all about it. Start at the beginning and let it all come out."

She treated me to another deep breath, complete with a sigh. I was so wrapped up in the compassionate mode that I forgot to check the cleavage.

"You are quite right Harry," she began, in a steadier voice, "I have to put my trust in someone like you. Forgive me for being so hesitant, but it has all been so frightening and sinister. I haven't known what to do. I do need a pair of strong shoulders to take over the terrible responsibility of this awful business.

"Well I offer you mine," trying for a hint of nonchalant bravado, but I'll admit I was getting worried. I'm not keen on responsibilities, especially terrible ones...probably why I'm not married.

"There is a life at stake here," she muttered in little more than a whisper.

"Whose?" I enquired.

"My husband's," she replied slowly. Then in a rush, as though she couldn't get it out fast enough. "He has been kidnapped."

No wonder the poor woman was so upset. My brain needed time: a brief moment to absorb the shock of such a shattering revelation. In an endeavour to buy it some time, I came out with pretty much the first things that came into my mind. "When, where, and how?"

No one had ever asked me for my assistance in a kidnapping case before; I was treading on virgin territory. Furthermore, I wasn't at all sure that my experience as a finder would be of much help. Most of my expertise has been scraped up in the pursuit of missing items. It is true; on the rare occasion, I have managed to flush out a missing person. Some of whom would have preferred to stay missing anyway. To be honest, and maybe heartless, missing persons are never worth the effort involved. There is more legwork to it, than profit.

Missing works of art now; well that's another ball game; has to be the most lucrative field in the finding business. Old paintings, antiques and the like seldom go missing in the sense of being mislaid. They are missing because some thieving hound made off with them; they get stolen! Quite often too, the loser has a pretty good idea of where their goods are heading...but they can't prove it. So really, those cases don't take a lot of head scratching on my part. I simply launch a reprisal raid, and pinch them back again. Surprisingly few people make a fuss, like calling in the police, when they discover that somebody has re-stolen their stolen goods. There is good money in it too, it really is amazing what people will pay to have some tatty old piece of bric-a-brac returned. This naturally, makes it a very appealing branch of the finding trade to me. Unfortunately, it does not provide a lot of opportunity to improve one's skills in the art of true detection.

So, I asked myself…was I qualified to take on a kidnapping case? The answer to that was a whopping NO.

But, then again…could I refuse a lady in distress? Certainly not: quite unthinkable.

On the other hand: "A life is at stake here," the Lady in distress had said. She was right, one false move on my part, and I'd have a death on my conscience.

Yet, couldn't a skilled and enterprising finder, maybe, just maybe come out of this: and looking good? If I could—the publicity would give my business a shove in the right direction. Might be the Finchley affair all over again; even better perhaps?

I was getting my thinking on the right track, things were looking possible. Then Lady Bexley began to answer my question of when, where, and how.

"I don't know exactly when it happened," she was saying. "It all started for me, as you can well imagine when I received the phone call. But that was two days after Sir Aubrey left here."

"Perhaps you could start somewhere close to the beginning Lady Bexley?" I enquired kindly, while doing my best not to look too puzzled. "From when you last saw your husband, I think might be about right. Which would be, I presume, before he left to go wherever he went?"

"Yes of course, quite right Harry. I accompanied him to the airport myself, you see."

I didn't, but I nodded wisely anyway. Then to get things going…"That sounds like a good place to start then."

She apparently agreed, for without a further prompting, but in a voice still heavy with emotion, these are the facts as she presented them to me.

Four days ago, which today being Friday, put it at Monday, her husband Sir Aubrey had departed on a business trip to Canada. His flight itinerary was via Toronto, with a final destination of Vancouver, British Columbia. Which explained her previous comment (the one she left hanging); about how interesting it was that I knew that city.

In Vancouver he had been scheduled to attend a meeting; "something to do with a mining consortium" where his presence was required for a couple of days.

For some reason, at this point in Lady Bexley's narrative, her emotions were bubbling to the surface. Tears began to well from her deep brown eyes. The sight of a tear slowly trickling down her cheek, I'm not ashamed to admit, raised a fair sized lump in my throat. This was the moment, I swear, when I decided to ignore the misgivings about my abilities, and jump into the kidnapped—victim recovery business with both feet. To hell with the consequences...this woman needed my help, and by crikey she was going to get it!

By this time however, Lady Bexley, had, with the aid of a lacy wisp of a handkerchief, taken care of the capricious tear. I'd had a poke around in my pocket for something to give her to mop up with, but could only detect a crumpled tissue so I abandoned the gesture.

With the lacy-wisp held at the ready, she went on to tell me in a confidential tone that Sir Aubrey had suggested how nice it would be if, when the business was concluded, she join him in Vancouver. "He tempted me with a cruise to Alaska," she said. "It was to be a second honeymoon," she added, which brought on more tears.

Another eye dabbing session followed, during which I fidgeted uncomfortably, and felt quite helpless.

"He never even got to that meeting," she went on pathetically. "And then," she sobbed, "I had that awful phone call."

"The ransom demand," I asked inanely, as though it wasn't bloody obvious.

"Yes," she bravely controlled her sobs, "two days ago, and it has seemed like a lifetime Harry."

"I'm sure it has," I commiserated. "Now, let's see what we can do about it. I realise how painful this is going to be, but tell me all you can remember about the call. Just take your time, and try to recall every detail, however unimportant it may seem."

"It will be painful, but I'll do my best," she said sitting up straighter. "I'll be all right now, thank you Harry. Please forgive me for giving way like that. I'm afraid, with not being able to tell anyone about this,

I have had it bottled up too long. I feel better already; now I've told you."

On that note she went on and told me about the phone call. Simply put, it went like this: The caller had informed her that her husband was being held, and had then outlined the terms of his release. She was instructed to get together a quantity of cut diamonds, the value of which should total £500,000.

Naturally, she said, she expressed doubts about that being possible. The caller then gave her precise details: the names of her husband's associates who could make the diamonds available, the colour and weight of the gems, together with other technicalities such as carats and points, which she was vague about and didn't mean much to me either.

It sounded as though the kidnappers knew a thing or two about diamonds.

Lady Bexley was then told to have the stones in her possession within twenty-four hours.

A further call yesterday had asked if these conditions had been met. She was able to confirm that they had.

She was at that time advised to have a messenger on hand, to affect the exchange, one person only; prepared to travel. The same threats were repeated concerning the life expectancy of the victim if the police were notified.

I realised that my decision to jump in with both feet, had been a case of jumping to conclusions. I wasn't going to be asked to match wits with a gang of kidnappers; I was going to be asked to become an errand-boy. In with two feet all right, in hiking boots. I wasn't sure how I felt; peeved or pleased. When I considered the diminishing responsibilities of being a mere messenger, my feelings were registering pleasure...so I left them there. I noticed that my shoulders were hardly sagging at all.

As Lady Bexley appeared to have reached the end of her narrative, I asked if she had received any further calls since yesterday.

"No, not a word from him," she replied, "and, as you can well imagine, I have been most reluctant to move away from the phone for too long. It was probably as well though, that he didn't choose to call again before I had this opportunity to talk with you."

She was getting that sad look back into her eyes again. I hoped mine weren't showing the relief I was feeling. This seemed like the right time to confirm my assessment of the situation, so I asked, "Am I to take it then Lady Bexley that you do wish me to act as the bearer of the ransom?"

She answered by reaching into her handbag and producing a suede leather bag. It was about the size of a marble bag I'd owned as a kid. Loosening the cord, she gently shook several diamonds onto the coffee table between us. The she looked up at me with a look of inquiry.

What could I say...I nodded acceptance.

After replacing the loose diamonds and pulling the drawstring tight, she pushed the pouch across the table towards me. "Better take them now Harry. After I get the next call you may have to be off in a hurry. I shall of course, call you as soon as I hear anything."

I suggested that as the kidnappers would be certain to give her adequate warning, and as she was only presuming the exchange rendezvous would be in Canada, there was no real need for me to take possession of the diamonds at this time.

She was quite adamant however; so I picked up the pouch and slipped it into my pocket, sensing as I did so, that naturally the one thing on Lady Bexley's mind was to get her husband back, safe and sound, and as soon as possible. Perhaps the main reason for her need, to hand the diamonds over to me now, was an unconscious desire to speed things up towards that end.

Using her phone, I arranged a round-the-clock answering service, and gave her the number.

As I was preparing to leave, we discussed various aspects of the situation. During which time I did my best to allay her fears by endeavouring to providing encouragement, optimism, and not least...confidence in her choice of a ransom bearer. She in turn lightened my heart by suggesting a fee for my services. A very generous fee it was too, £3,000 when the ransom was delivered…regardless of the outcome. Also, she informed me that the envelope which she handed me, as I took my leave, contained a similar amount in cash to cover my travelling expenses. I was beginning to feel a fondness towards my new client.

CHAPTER TWO

The sun was shining as I descended the twenty-foot wide stone steps and walked to my parked Bentley. Sliding behind the wheel; firing the old girl up and burbling off along the driveway; I could not help but feel that the day was shaping up nicely.

Sparing a cheery nod to the statues (the gardeners must have been on their tea break) I drove out of the gates, made a right turn, worked my way up through the gears and let the events of the day trickle through my mind.

Considering that the day started off with a hangover, and then had got a tad gut wrenching through the emotional stuff, with the sad Lady Bexley...sobbing women do it to me every time. Add to that the disappointment of not landing the starring role, and then the relief of not getting lumbered with the kidnapping recovery lark, well things were not looking too bad at all!

Nice straight job of work; I mean, it wasn't going to give the old grey matter a rupture. No problems, that I could foresee—well, perhaps the odd one might rear its head, like getting the diamonds into Canada. I could hardly declare them, I mused…but then revealing all to Customs types, would hardly give me heart palpitations; it never has.

No, there was hardly a problem in sight. Somebody was even going to tell me where to find this joker. All I had to do was go and buy him back; purchase price provided.

What could be easier? Here I am I thought…toddling along, the sun is shining; I've got a pocket full of diamonds and a comforting wad of folding money to get me wherever I need to go. "Sit back and relax Harry old cock," I told myself.

For a drive through the countryside; the road I was on would be hard to beat. An interesting assortment of curves and hills, as it wound its way through the rural scenery of Kent. The gearbox on the Bentley was getting a good workout, and I was taking pleasure in making the changes smooth. I had the road to myself…ahead of me that is. There was one other car behind me, cluttering up my rear view mirror.

It seemed to be pacing me, a grey Morris Minor at a distance of about hundred yards or so. Probably admiring the Bentley, or contemplating giving me a contest. Funny, how a car like mine will bring out the competitive spirit of small car drivers. They just love to show me their arse-ends. Now there are the odd female rear-ends, which are a definite treat to be behind…but the prospect of viewing the disappearing butt of a Morris does not fall into that category.

So I decided to find out what the intentions might be. I gave the gas pedal a little more weight…to make things interesting. The old girl's tires began to voice their protest as they scrabbled to hang on to the curves. But the Morris, being a lot handier at that caper stayed right with me…same distance.

So, another test was called for, which might reveal some intentions. I beetled round the next bend in a real hurry; then trod on the anchors, which shortened the distance between us dramatically. Gave me the chance to see who was in the other car; two chaps up front was about all I could make out from the reflection in the rear view mirror. They made no effort to pass me, so I ruled out arse-flashing.

Were they following me? I asked myself. Easy to find out; I goosed the gas pedal briefly; then pulled well over to give them room to pass me. The Morris simply adjusted to the hundred yard gap again, which more or less answered my question...it wanted to follow me.

Next question; why? Another easy one to find the answer to...ask them! I pulled onto the verge of the road, and stopped.

Obligingly, the other car also stopped. But the gap between us had shortened; it was down to about twenty yards.

I kept my eyes on the rear view mirror. The driver stayed put, but the door opened on the passenger's side. A chap got out...he was wearing a Balaclava helmet or a ski mask...not something you'd see everyday in a country lane in Kent.

Slipping the gear stick into reverse, I popped the clutch...and went sailing backwards.

The poor sods didn't stand a chance. A couple of tons of extremely well put together motor car hit that little car with a crunching impact.

I had my door open, and came out on the run before the two vehicles came to a complete stop.

The passenger had been well and truly belted by the door he had been about to swing open. He had been deposited some distance back from his starting point. He was lying on his back, half on the verge and half in the bushes, but I could see his open eyes through the mask.

I gave the driver a quick glance; he wasn't wearing a mask so I could see the blood on his face. His eyes were closed...I diagnosed that he had lost interest in the proceedings.

Turning back to the chap laying on the grass and bushes, I noted that the bushes were stinging nettles. The least of his problems I thought...he looked decidedly shop-worn.

"Good afternoon," I remarked in a sociable manner. "You look as though you've had a bit of an accident."

"Jesus bloody Christ," he muttered.

Clearly, he was not amused. Moving slowly, he propped himself up on his hands and knees.

"If you are going to fidget mate, do it very slowly." I suggested. "Just keep your hands where they are—flat on the ground."

He either hadn't been listening, or my message wasn't clear to him, or he felt like living recklessly? Whatever the reason for his lack of prudence…he made a lunge for my ankle.

However, his reflexes were painfully slow, so I had all kinds of time to take a step backwards, and then give him a boot alongside where I thought his ear should be. My best Oxfords, which I had chosen to wear this morning, are quite a sturdy shoe. Heavy enough, I would have thought to set his reflexes back another notch.

Even so, he looked as though he might be contemplating another grab, but common sense prevailed and he placed both his hands on the ground in front of him.

As he did so I seized the opportunity of leaning forward, whipping a hand to the top of his mask, and yanking it off his head.

Fair headed bloke, a bit older than me, say thirty something. He stared at me, a hard defiant look; about as defiant a look as a chap can manage when his hair is standing on end. Snatching the mask off his head had not done a thing for his hairdo. Even so, I could tell he wasn't about to blow me a kiss.

Just as I was contemplating what line of chatter to pursue, he pulled his lips back to show me some teeth, and snarled. "You stupid bungling idiot, you've just signed the old mans death warrant."

Giving me another hint about what was going on. "Oh, which old man would that be?" I probed.

"Bexley you flaming moron. Sir bloody Bexley, who else."

To say I was bewildered would be a considerable understatement. But in my line of business it's best not to show it. I kept my poker face in place, and as I was short on information, where anything he might say could be a bonus, I decided to waffle on a bit. "I'm not sure I'm quite with you," I tried for openers.

"Piss off mate!"

Not too productive! Take a sharper mind than mine, to get anything helpful out of that. It did give me a hunch though that he was already regretting having said as much as he had.

Obviously I was face to face with the kidnappers, or at least one who was connected to them. What to do now, I pondered? I could boot him in the other ear, entreating him to reveal all. He looked a tough sod though, and I doubted if he would cough up much. Time too, was a factor; the road wasn't going to stay deserted forever. I scratched the interrogation idea. I had a better one. Run the facts of life past him. Who knows, I might get the starring role after all.

"Listen to me," I told him. "I'll spell things out for you slowly. I appreciate that your noggin has been rattled, but in your own interests do try to follow what I am about to say. Now, as I see it, you want something that I have. Yes I do have the diamonds; note the emphasis is on the first person, it is me, Harry Potts you have to deal with now. Lady Bexley has commissioned me as her agent. However, I think you will find me quite accommodating…if I am approached in the right way. Which means, don't come skulking up behind me in a bloody Morris, right? Now to the nitty-gritty, the only way you'll get a pay day is to hand Sir Bexley over to me. I am not the law…far from it, so the fact that I can identify you is not important. I suggest also, that if you play your cards right, you're onto a good thing. Produce the victim in good condition, and the diamonds are all yours. If not, well tough shit old son. I'll tell you something else too, which you'd do well to consider. I don't give a tinker's toss either way; I've never met Sir Bexley, and I won't be weeping into my pillow if I never do. I'm being paid; win lose or draw. So you just make your phone call when you're ready, and we'll get down to doing business." I had been backing up as I delivered that spiel, and as I opened my car door, I called out "Have a nice day"

I took off in a spray of gravel, while he got to his feet mouthing something that the roar of the Bentley's exhaust muffled.

I knew the Morris wasn't going to follow me anymore, its radiator had been quietly hissing all through my impromptu dissertation. I was confident that it had been mortally wounded. I was a bit less confident about the results my gush of words might precipitate.

In the heat of the moment, especially as I had a captive audience so to speak, my line of patter had seemed reasonably logical. Now that the moment had passed however, I wasn't quite as sure.

It has however, always been my way…in like Flynn and let the dust settle where, or on, whom it may.

Usually, it will provoke some line of action, and as they say (whoever they may be) "something moving is something happening."

As I debated the possibility of a large portion of the dust settling on me, I also gave some thought to the intriguing puzzle of how Whosit and Whatsit (the two in the Morris), had got onto me so quickly. I determined that the least I could do after possibly disturbing a hornet's nest by bashing a car and booting an ear, was to make some effort at finding out.

Stopping at the next phone box I spotted, I dialled the Bexley number. Lady Bexley, obviously at the ready, answered on the second ring. I hastened to assure her that all was well, but I understood that it was her secretary who had made the call to me, and I wondered if she had been privy to the kidnapping? Or, were any of the staff, (like the butler for instance), aware of the situation?

She assured me that neither her secretary, nor any member of her household staff knew anything about "this distressing business." Although; Lady Bexley said, she had considered taking her secretary Grace Watkins into her confidence, in fact, had Grace been at the Hall today while I was there she might have done so.

"Grace then, doesn't live at the Hall?" I asked her.

"No, she has her own little place in Tunbridge Wells."

"That's nice," I commented. "Well you sound as though you are in better spirit, which really is the purpose of this call. I was a little worried about you when I left. You'll call me as soon as you hear anything?"

"The very minute," she replied. "And thank you so much for your concern Harry. I'm pleased, that you are such a caring person."

Devious would be closer I thought, as I went through the motions of tapering the conversation off, saying goodbye, then hanging up the phone.

Pity she's married, I idly conjectured, as I thumbed through the directory before leaving the phone booth. I could be tempted in her direction. And, I thought to myself, one can't pick a much better time to fool around with a married woman, than when her husband is being held to ransom…especially when I've got the ransom.

Chiding myself for having such delicious thoughts, while urging myself to stick to business, I ran my finger down the appropriate listing and noted the number of one Grace Watkins.

Twenty minutes later, I was standing in front of her door. I used the knocker, a lion's head with a ring and a clapper through its nose. The opening door also opened the curtain on an extremely proportioned pair of mammary glands; the like of which a chap would walk all day, just to get a glimpse of. Restrained under a sweater, and pointing straight at me, they looked to me like they were begging to be liberated.

Forcing my eyes upwards…which required considerable effort. I saw lips that promised better things than the mere forming of words. I saw hair, two-tone blonde hair, framing blue eyes flecked with a dash of mischief, in a cheeky face.

The lips proved they could manage to form words quite well too, giving me a demonstration by saying, "Can I help you?"

Could she help me! My mind was busy sifting options, but my voice stuck to business. "My name is Harry Potts. You had occasion to call me yesterday on behalf of Lady Bexley."

"That's right, I did," she said, with a ripple of a frown playing across her brow. "Nothing wrong I hope?"

"Should there be?" I asked.

Her lips compressed. She looked at a loss for words, which proved to be right because I didn't get any.

"Look," I went on. "Do you suppose I could come in? I'd like to talk to you."

She pulled the door open wider. "Of course, I'm sorry, yes, do come in."

Showing me in, she gestured towards a chair. "Have a seat please. I have just made myself some coffee, would you care for a cup?"

"Nice of you, thank you."

I lowered myself into the chair, while she stepped into a small alcove, chatting politely over the clatter of cups on saucers. This was a step saving flat, she told me; twenty steps from the front door took you out of the back door. As I listened to how small, and nice, and how convenient the flat was, I looked about me.

She was right; it was nice. Tastefully decorated, nicely furnished with smaller pieces which didn't crowd the small area, neatly kept, and all with an air of femininity.

Emerging from the small alcove with a tray, she set the coffee on a small table. I looked at her closely as she sat across from me. Taking a sip of her coffee, Grace returned my scrutiny over the rim of her cup, and met my eyes steadily.

"Now," she said seriously, "What would you like to talk to me about?"

"A question first, if I may," I began. "Did Lady Bexley happen to mention why she wanted to get in touch with me?"

"No, she didn't Mr. Potts. Something is wrong, isn't it?"

"Call me Harry," I said. "What makes you think anything is wrong?"

"All right Harry. You're a policeman, aren't you?"

"What makes you think that?"

"Because, you keep answering a question with another one, you just did it again. Anyway, I rather hope you are."

"Why."

She answered that with a raised shoulders and open palms gesture, while retorting. "If you aren't a policeman, then I'm not going to answer that question."

"Very well Miss Watkins…"

She interrupted, "Call me Grace."

We traded half smiles…and I did some thinking. Dilemma time, if she is on the right side of the fence, yet suspects that all is not well at Weald Hall; she may just go to the police. That scenario would not suit me at all. I decided to use my 'Special Branch' routine.

"As I was about to say Grace, I can see that I must take you into my confidence. Come clean, as we say in the trade. Mine is a special branch of the law, (like Murphy's Law, I thought) and I must ask you to keep that confidential. Let me just assure you though, that anything you say to me will cause no harm to the Bexleys."

The stubborn, even belligerent, set of her lips began to soften. Then, with what sounded like a sigh of relief, she said, "You know,

I've been trying to decide all day whether I should go to the police. I just knew something was wrong."

"Rest easy, we have the matter in hand. Unfortunately, it's not possible at this time for me to disclose anymore than that. What made you suspect that something was…shall we say, amiss?"

"I suppose, because Lady Helen has been acting out of character. Yet, when I asked her if anything was wrong, she went to such lengths to convince me that nothing was, that she in fact confirmed that something had to be. I knew all right…but I took the easy way out and decided it wasn't my business. And I'm not proud of that."

"I quite understand." I commiserated. "But don't feel too bad about it, you did the right thing. Any input from you, however helpful your intentions, could well have aggravated things. As you have surmised, there is a problem, which unfortunately has yet to be resolved. So your best bet now, if you want to help, is to carry out your duties as normally and as naturally as you can. With that in mind, I'm sure you will agree it will be best if you don't mention our conversation to Lady Bexley."

She nodded her head so emphatically, her hair bounced.

"One more thing I wanted to ask you," I said. "Try to remember if there have been any strangers about the Hall lately: tradesmen, repair people, anyone like that."

She sat; elbows on knees, giving that some thought, the while alternating a caress of her cup, with a sip of her coffee. "The phone people were in last week," she mused. "Checking out the lines…I think they said."

Well, now I knew how they knew.

Feeling a smirk of satisfaction coming on, I decided it was time to relax a little. "O K Grace, now that I've confided in you, would you be prepared to help me?"

"I'll do anything I can, very willingly," she replied eagerly. "Just tell me what you want me to do."

"Then how about a little undercover assignment?" I asked, with a lift of my eyebrows"

"Really…undercover eh! Gosh, that sounds exciting, tell me more."

"Right; not terrible exciting though, but when you go about your duties at the Hall, I'd like you to keep your eyes and ears open. Then let me know if you see, hear, or sense anything out of the ordinary."

"Like what?"

"Good question," I mused. "I don't know what. We'll have to rely on your intuitions, anything out of the ordinary, is about all I can tell you. If you do come up with something, however trivial it may appear on the surface—call me."

"All right, I'll do that."

"Oh yes, there is one other thing," I said seriously.

"Really," she said matching my sombre look.

"I've been using my eyes, ears, and senses while I have been sitting here, and they have been telling me how stunningly attractive you are, so the other thing is, will you have dinner with me this evening?"

She put down her cup and rested her hands on her knees, which she managed to make look like a fondle and then looked at me pensively for a few moments. Then she switched her eyes to twinkle, and her vocal chords to melodious chuckle. In between chuckles, she managed, "And there I was, all keyed up, waiting for the cloak and dagger stuff."

"So get your cloak on, recommend the rendezvous, and I imagine the waiter will provide a dagger of sorts."

"You win," she said, still having a little chuckle. "Give me a few minutes to do something with my face, and I'll be right with you." As she retreated from the room, she added. "Try the Mucky Duck, the number is in my book, just there by the phone."

I called the White Swan, which I knew would be the listed name of the Duck (that cute English sense of humour) and booked a table.

On her return to the room she was saying, "Get the Duck all right?"

I noticed she had exchanged the sweater for an open necked white blouse—with a view.

Tearing my eyes away from the scenery, I threw her a nod regarding the Duck.

"They do a nice Smorg, I hope you'll like it," she was saying as she pulled on a coat.

26

"Dutch-treat if I don't," I smiled.

"Not on your Nellie; after the way you tricked me into it—you carrot dangler," she said. "All right, I'm ready if you are."

I was certainly ready…but I'm patient. "Off we go then," was what I said.

She locked the door, and then I led her to the car and held the door for her.

"My, my," she remarked as I slipped in beside her. "Your Special Branch, are not stingy are they?"

"Actually," I replied, "this is part of my upper-crust investigating kit. I ride a bike most of the time, which will give you an idea about the level of my usual cases. However, no more shop talk. Direct me to your Mucky Duck."

CHAPTER THREE

With Grace directing and entertaining me with snippets of local knowledge, it seemed no more than a few minutes before our destination hove into view.

The Mucky Duck, which I know from patronising many White Swan's, in many locales, is no reflection on the establishment's housekeeping. This one turned out to be a country pub, which at a rough guess couldn't have been much more than four hundred years old.

I parked the Bentley in a cobble-stoned yard at the rear of the main building. In what was I imagined the stagecoach courtyard in bygone years.

We were early for our reservation so we decided to have a drink at the bar.

Country pubs are no longer the quiet retreat of yore…or even yesterday. The jukebox was cranking out, at full volume, a chorus of young male voices that hadn't broken yet, and it sounded a painful business! Tonight I would have opted for a selection of dreamy melodies, softly played...an aid to chatting up the fair damsel. I have no qualms about mixing business with pleasure, or vice versa for that matter.

The decibel count that was pounding our ears was a definite hindrance to the pursuit of my intentions. Chatting was out.

A group of loudmouths were horsing it up in the vicinity of the source of the music, an area that housed the jukebox and several slot machines. The few locals were engaged in the fixed-grin game of pretending not to notice the general bedlam.

I ushered Grace to the furthest end of the bar and called for our drinks, which took some shouting, mixed with a dash of sign language. Grace and I raised our glasses, and mouthed "Cheers" to each other. We propped ourselves up to the bar and contented ourselves with exchanging the occasional smile.

Then the noise factor changed, and not for the better. Looking over my shoulder I saw one of the group, was shaking and thumping a pin-machine. The increase in the noise level was also added to, by the yells of encouragement he was getting from his companions.

Dramatically, the music came to a sudden end, the yelling died down; the peace was heavenly.

"Well, hello there," I said to Grace. Then I glanced at the landlord behind the bar, observing that it was he who had committed the mercy killing...by the flick of a switch.

With his finger still poised over the switch, he shouted, "That's it lads. Drink up, then let's be having you out."

This did not go down well with the 'lads'.

Who were quick with their comments over the dastardly deed he had perpetrated. Shouted advice was aimed in the landlord's direction, mainly directing him to "Drop dead," "Get stuffed," and of course the usual referral to the do-it-yourself sexual intercourse. That one topped the polls in the repetition count.

It did cross my mind (briefly) to walk over and bang a few heads, but I allowed the thought the freedom to flutter away. Being, as I am, a cautious and responsible person, I was aware of the diamonds nestling in my pocket. Not to mention the money, and I have been hit hard enough in the past to knock money out of my pocket…come to think of it though, that was loose change in a trouser pocket. However, I joined the locals in playing the "I'm not here" game.

"You are a lot of loudmouthed louts. You should be ashamed of yourselves." Those words came from Grace…not what I needed!

Her voice carried astonishingly well…perfect diction.

The attention swung in her direction, and as I stood next to her, encompassed me with the menace of a Browning gun turret.

I eased out in front of Grace; not my first choice, just that my mind failed to come up with an alternative option. One of the group detached himself from the others; adopted a menacing posture and moved towards me.

I pasted on my most disarming smile and moved towards him. Most people, I have found are reluctant to punch a grinning face. I have been wrong on the odd occasion! I studied the approaching threat while awaiting his arrival. I would have wished for a smaller bloke, but then, sometimes they are faster…nothing's perfect.

As he loomed closer, my smile got harder to keep pasted in place. This guy had a lot going for him: tall, heavily muscled, mean looking, and with his tattooed arms akimbo I felt as though a mobile bill-board was about to run me down.

He was taking his time, or perhaps time was standing still; it can do so on these occasions. I had time to observe all details, from his Western boots up. The boots looked like size twelve; he wouldn't be easy to knock off his feet. Tight trousers displayed some useful thigh muscles. A wide, big buckled belt added decoration to his slacks, which were tight enough to look glued on, they certainly had no need of a belt to keep them up. The black leather jacket had the sleeves cut off, the better to show his tattoos. There were enough metal studs on the jacket to make a trip to the scrap yard a profitable venture. He had a mop of hair which looked like "before" in a shampoo advertisement. A Charlie Chan moustache that most of us wouldn't be caught dead wearing; but it suited him.

He blew it forward as he said. "If you're with that mouthy bitch, sod your luck."

I thought he was probably right.

He stopped some four feet in front of me. Still smiling (he must have had me pegged as the village idiot) I very slowly moved my hand up to rub the side of my nose.

His eyes were following my hand as the toe of my shoe slammed into his—shall we say soft underbelly, but slightly lower? The target had been well accented by those tight jeans. From four feet away, with the height just right, it was like kicking a soccer ball on the volley. Perfect distance, maximum momentum on contact, I'd felt my shoe hit bone.

His reaction was predictable and completely understandable. Pain erased all other thoughts from his mind, except the one instinct which told him he had to get his knees up. He put on a commendable performance as he slowly jack-knifed to the floor, fell on his side and pulled himself into the fetal position.

The silence, broken only by the unhappy warrior's grunts and groans was, for want of a better word, charged.

I thought the chap's performance a touch on the dramatic side; if he was looking for sympathy he wasn't getting it from me. I looked at his troops with raised eyebrows.

One of them looked like he might be pumping himself up, so I gave him one of my cold-eyed stares. "Don't be tempted mate," I cautioned, "I'm still rarin' to go. Your mate looks as though he could use a bit of fresh air, do yourself a favour and lug him outside."

Fortunately, without Charlie Chan, the starch seemed to have gone out of them. I'd be a blockhead if I said I wasn't totally grateful when they chaired away the main performer. A sneak attack is one thing; a pitched battle would have set my good health back painfully. I had a mental picture of me being carted out through that same door on a stretcher…but then, it doesn't do to dwell on the "might have been."

I wandered back to the bar and Grace, sank the last inches of my beer, and then asked her, "Like another to celebrate the coming of peace?"

Before she could answer, the landlord interrupted. "These are on the house, I'm indebted to you. Not that I encourage violence in the house, but that crowd needed sorting out."

"Same again then," I said looking at Grace.

She nodded to the landlord, and then said to me "It was hardly fair to kick him like that."

. "Good thing you weren't the referee then," I frowned at her. "You might have disqualified me. What are you then, a Queensbury fan? Those rules don't apply anymore, gone are the days when gents sloshed each other across the chops with their gloves."

"Still wasn't fair, "she repeated.

Funny, how non-participants in a fracas, invariably get snotty if you deviate from what they call fair play. What rubbish…had I taken up a fighting stance, blood and snot would have been flying all over the place, and most of it would have been mine. We'd have been dancing all over the bar, and God knows what might have happened to the diamonds. I could even have wound up under arrest if the brawl had gone on long enough. That's saying nothing about the energy waste; I'm only counting mine. Talking of energy, I'd take bets Fog-brain in the tight pants wouldn't be expending any energy tonight, or for many nights to come. Who knows, I might have done my bit towards slowing down the population explosion!

"At least you did something." Grace interrupted my rambling thoughts. "I was beginning to think there wasn't a red blooded male in the place."

"Fat chance you gave me, and I didn't exactly attack the clot. Anyway, who started it?"

"Maybe I just wanted to just see what you would do. Wondered if you might arrest them, you are a bit of a mystery man to me; perhaps a riddle which I'd enjoy solving."

I brightened up, "I'll make that easy for you, I volunteered, and give you all the help I can. There are however much pleasanter ways of getting to know me. You didn't have to toss me into the arena. The only thing you learned from which," I offered sarcastically, "is that I'm unfair."

"Oh, I wouldn't say that. I learned that you are a man quite able to take care of himself. Although, dare I say it, the method was…unconventional? Unconventional and intriguing, will you settle for that?"

"Hmm, yes I guess so. If that means you want to get to know me better. I give you fair warning…I plan on enlarging my knowledge of you."

She looked at me a long moment, took a sip of her drink; then with that mischievous twinkle back in her eyes, said, "Do you indeed? Enlarge your knowledge, eh? You're teasing me again Harry, do I detect a note of lechery? Are you by any chance, referring to carnal knowledge?"

"Absolutely," I said. "You're right on the button." Then, before I had time to capitalise on the favourable direction the conversation had taken, the waiter signalled that our table was ready for us.

As soon as we were seated however, and I had selected the wine, I gave the turn of events a not so subtle nudge. "Right then, and to get back to your question on carnal knowledge"

"You're impatient too, Harry," she said, smiling sweetly. "See how much I'm learning about you?" she added archly. "Tell me about you're appetite, and I'm talking about food."

I gave her a wry grin, as I escorted her towards the food. The selection was vast. No small wonder that Grace had confidently recommended it. Moving along the laden tables we heaped our plates from the offerings. Nothing wrong with her appetite!

Carrying the spoils back to our table, I launched a further push towards picking up the threads of our verbal intercourse. "We were almost discussing carnal whatnot," I prompted her.

"Well, I knew it would come up sooner or later," she said. "So, not being one to beat about the bush, I thought I'd enquire what your intentions were!"

"Were, and are, to save a lot of bush pruning."

"Yes, well I like what I see too, so…" she let that hang while popping a radish into her mouth. "We shall just have to wait and see, won't we?"

Which to me was as good as a promise although tentative; of

things to come. With that settled; as though by mutual accord, we relaxed and talked our way through dinner.

We traded likes and dislikes. I offered a few bits about myself, not much information and not all of that true. I still felt the need to keep my cover story, so I wove some larger than life public relations around it.

In exchange, Grace sketched me a scanty picture of her background. Born and raised in Kent. An only child, both parents departed. Whether they had done a bunk, gone on holiday, or were deceased she didn't say, and I didn't pry. She moved to London after finishing a course on business management, but was not enamoured with city life. A country girl at heart? Speaking of the heart she confided; she had had a few affairs of the body, but her heart was still a virgin. I mentally conceded that not too many of us were perfect...but I was not nutty enough to say it.

She had been with the Bexleys only a short time, and loved working for them.

I was onto that in a flash, and determined that a short time was less than five months.

From then on the conversation flowed on, running over generalities that didn't need to much thinking about. I was, in fact, idly picking up the vibes coming from her, and my antennae was receiving satisfactory signals.

Conversation really bubbled now at a bright level throughout the meal; which, incidentally, was excellent.

We drove back to Grace's flat, with a distinct feeling of closeness, the touch of knees, the brush of a hand on arm...promising body language?

I walked with her to the front door. Turning the key in the lock she turned to me; took my hand and said. "Come in Harry."

I didn't have to be dragged through the doorway, and I adroitly back-heeled the door shut after me.

The glow from the street lights filtering in through the window, bathed the room in a soft glow. I couldn't have asked for more, if I'd arranged the setting.

She didn't turn on the light, simply stood facing me; with her arms at her sides, handbag still dangling from one hand. I've seldom had a nicer invitation.

I put my hands on her hips and gently pulled her close to me. My lips found hers. We held the kiss while our bodies basked in each other's warmth. My arms had completely encircled her slender waist; I heard her handbag thud on the floor, then her arms were around my neck.

"Harry darling." she whispered; her voice husky…"I think we had better cool off."

Her words slowly sank into my brain, and were as welcome as a bucket of ice water. Maybe, my brain argued; this was a "Stop it, I like it" message. My brain and I have run into that experience before. Sometimes a lady likes to make you appear to be the aggressor (very nice it is too) so that should things misfire, they can play hell. And, she did call me 'darling'. Press on Harry, I decided, give it your best shot!

"Grace, the temperature is just fine, hot is good."

"But, we've only known each other a few hours," she murmured. "I do want you to be close to me, I think you can tell that. It's, just well…I think we should see each other a few more times; get to know each other better, before we get carried away."

"Only a few hours Grace," I said. "I feel I've known you all my life," which is a line that has produced good results in the past.

"Oh Harry," she sighed. "I feel that way too. I think I could fall in love with you, which is why I want us to wait a while."

"You're right," I lied. "Let's sit down a minute and get to know each other." Nothing like a little anticipation to increase the appetite!

"I had a little longer than that in mind," she laughed. "No we'll say goodnight, and give ourselves a bit longer."

"Like tomorrow night?" I suggested.

"Don't you have something else to do?"

"Yes, but I don't have anyone to do it with."

"You have a one track mind Harry…I was referring to the case, investigation, or whatever you call it."

"Yes, I know…better pay attention to business. I'm depending on you though to stay close to me on that too. But, as they say, all work and no play, and I'd rather play with you anytime. You have my number, so if you can't sleep, don't hesitate"

"Go home Harry," she laughed.

So I left, after a peck of a kiss that she didn't allow to linger.

CHAPTER FOUR

Grace, with her arm waving, disappeared into the night as I eased the Bentley away from her flat.

A glance at my watch as I accelerated onto the main road, confirmed that with some low flying I could reach my local pub before closing time.

Small consolation, I thought, for my early dismissal by teasing Grace. I'd really thought I was set there for the night, but that's a woman for you. Sometimes I think I'll never understand them. My mind boggled, when I summarised. Girl with her own flat, the place to ourselves; nice evening spent together; excellent dinner; scintillating conversation; physical awareness; perfect situation…should have been, target for tonight-bombs away.

Instead—operation scrub…big fat zero!

Wonder why girls have to feel they have to get to know you better? Better than what, a big contradiction really. Logically, a kiss and a cuddle is a great and proven way to get to know each other better.

Tossed that thought around for a while, without finding a flaw in it. Then my subconscious poked an oar in, suggesting that I was making excuses, when the bottom line was…I had lost my touch, but I didn't listen to that line of thought. Law of averages, some you win…some are still to be won.

About half way through the journey home, I shelved the mystery of women. Which wasn't bad; some idiots have spent a lifetime on that riddle…then died wondering.

I turned my mind to the case in hand, more to the point—the events of the day that I allowed to run past in review. I find it often helps me to unravel other people's devious minds. Little things; that when recalled, just don't have the right ring to them.

The tearful Lady Bexley, relating the kidnapping tale, was the beginning, so I started the replay there…and immediately registered an off-key note. All that stuff about Sir Bexley's associates, making available the right kind and value of diamonds? Smelled a bit fishy to me?

That had to be someone who knew plenty about "old Bexley" as the lad in the Balaclava had called him. Lady Bexley hadn't mentioned anything about her husband being old, had she? But then, no reason why she should, I had naturally paired her up with someone about her own age. Lesson there; do not presume.

That thought reminded me that I had failed to ask her for a photograph of her husband. Whoops…very remiss Harry. If I wanted to come out of this looking good, buying back the wrong bloke was not going to do it for me.

All extremely confusing, I had a lot of loose ends hanging about, without much idea of how to tie them together.

The Morris bashing incident? That was like something out of Comic Cuts…even the News of the World would think twice about running that story!

Then, even if, as I had deduced from what Grace told me, there was a tap on the Bexley phone line, how did the duo in the Morris know that Lady Bexley had handed me the diamonds? I had been reluctant to take them, and could easily have told her to hang on to them—so where did that leave me?

My mind wandered off again, finding its way back to the chap in the Morris. Which gave me a chuckle; I could still see his face when I whipped that hood off. I wondered what his next move would be.

Then, things came into perspective. What the hell was I trying to gather up all those loose ends for? None of it mattered, I'd tossed the ball into the kidnapper's court, and what options did they have. They could kill Bexley and call it a day…too bad for him; case closed for me. They could call Lady Bexley and tell her they didn't much care for her choice of messenger…case closed for me. They could call me…a free trip for me.

No sense in worrying about which way the ball was going to bounce back.

But, for all that, I was still seeking answers as I pulled into the parking area of the Rose and Crown my local pub. With ten minute to go before closing time, I beetled in for a quick pint.

The Rose as it is known by its patrons, has been my watering-hole, from the time I moved into the village of Sterling Minnis; some years ago. I came here after my demob from the RAF, at the end of the war, and have had (as yet) no urge to go elsewhere.

The Rose is a real country pub. It was when it was built in the year of 1697, and it still is today. There have, I'm sure, been a few changes made to the building and its surroundings. Where the cars are parked now, was without doubt a space for horse drawn carriages. But it was built as a place of hospitality, and so it remains, a comfortable haven for genial conversation. A neutral meeting place for neighbours, where all are welcomed as guests. Fred the landlord is our host; he is also our arbiter; friend, and occasionally our referee.

As I stepped through the door the usual assortment of regulars were pursuing their various activities. Two pairs at the dartboard, chucking darts, while chatting and deducting scores at the speed of an adding machine. A few were at a table playing dominoes—more like a tableau in suspended animation than an activity; a group at the bar sharing a laugh with Fred, who by reflex was pulling me a pint.

Chalky was perched on his throne; a stool at the end of the bar, where he was leaning his bulk against the wall.

"Evening all," I announced, accepting my pint from Fred as I passed. Moving along beside Chalky's perch I raised my glass in greeting and got a nod in reply.

I'd expected him to be here; Friday night is one he seldom misses. I looked at him as I slid enough beer down to let my throat know that all was well with the world.

Bertram White; inevitably known as Chalky, in his sixties and wearing his years lightly. Corrugated hair, a full head of it, short back and sides of course, and still blonde enough to hide the grey, a ruddy complexion on a face weathered by many years of exposure. A hard face when he wasn't smiling. An ex-policeman's enquiring eyes—not an easy man to lie to. I can vouch for that, I tried, before I got to know him well.

He was smiling now. "Well young fella, been chasing some poor lass around a haystack have you?"

He was trying to wind me up, probably because he knew I seldom come to the Rose this late. I'm usually here for the evening, or not at all

"You know me better than that Chalky," I retorted. "I'd have let her catch me, then I wouldn't have been here at all."

"Humph, I know you all right. Must have been some husband came home early. Hopped out of the window, did you? Bloody tomcat you are son. Do yourself a mischief one of these days, the way you carry on."

"Envy will get you nowhere," I pointed out. "If you want to know the fact of the matter, I terminated a torrid evening, and rushed back here just so I could enjoy your astonishing if somewhat inaccurate wit."

"Glad you enjoy it," he commented wryly.

"I also hoped you could dig into your probably ill-gotten store of knowledge and offer me some advice."

"Oh yes, got something on then, have we?" His face didn't give him away, but his rhythm changed. He lifted his glass to take a swig, forgot the swig, and put his glass down again…he was excited, I know him well.

We'd met when he was still new to retirement, and I was new to the finding game. In fact, I don't think I would have had much success without him. The bonus in our relationship is that we have become friends. Perhaps, because of the difference in our ages, we have donned the roles of father and son. I don't know; except he didn't have a son nor I a father. Could be we have developed that kind of bond, without the inhibitions quite often associated with it.

As I hadn't answered him he couldn't curb his curiosity. Draining his glass, he thumped it down on the bar, rubbed his hands together and prompted: "Well tell me about it then, don't just stand there contemplating your navel."

"This one is different, very hush-hush," I said it in an appropriately lowered voice, and with a flick of my eyes towards the group still laughing it up along the bar. "We'll talk at my place, OK?"

He nodded, while I pushed our glasses forward as a signal to Fred the landlord. "Just time for another," I said as he picked up the glasses.

"How's it going Harry" said Fred as he set the refilled glasses back in front of us. "Giving the lads a break tonight," glancing over at the dart players, "you were on top form last night, it was just like your arrows had radar."

'The way it goes, right...some nights you can't lose for winning. The arrangement about the phone all right, usual drill—contact me or Chalky?"

"Oh yeah, no trouble, got a phone in the bedroom now, so anytime is okay. Well almost," he mused, "If you interrupt anything intimate, it'll cost you an extra bob or two."

The Rose is also my twenty four hour a day answering service.

Sensing that Chalky was champing at the bit, and as I wasn't disposed to hurry my drink, I switched to his favourite topic.

"How's the steam locomotive coming along?" I tempted him.

I had his attention instantly. After his retirement from London's Metropolitan Police Force, and his move to "the country" as he likes to put it, he had set his garage up as a machine shop. In this, he has passed his time in the making of a model steam locomotive. I have watched it develop from a package of rough castings; some bits of scrap steel plate and some odd lengths of copper and brass pipe. He is well on the way, in the production of a four foot long replica of one of the crack locomotives he remembers from his boyhood. This little work of art, will, he assures me, burn coal to get up steam, with which, it will transport up to four people along a track.

That is, if he gets it right. I kid him; if he gets it wrong he could blow the poor buggers up.

"Coming along nicely," said Chalky. "As a matter of fact; today was a big one. Motion work complete, valve gear timed, and get a load of this—she runs! Only on compressed air yet, of course, but the little sod goes. I tell you Harry, when I saw those pistons and wheels and connecting rods all moving together...well I was beside myself. It was a real treat, she runs like a sewing machine. You just wait; you'll be eating your words when you see me chuffing along a track."

"Really," I said. "You can bet I'll be eating them at a safe distance then...waiting for the bang. We'll all be calling you Sooty never mind Chalky, after the smoke clears."

Like most policemen he is a listener. Content to let you do the talking—while he waits for the inevitable slip of the tongue that will let him read between the lines. But, on the subject of his little engine, he is garrulous. So without the need for further input on my part, I was able to sit back with an eyebrow cocked, and look as though I was agog with interest and admiration, while enjoying my beer.

Not that I had long...I'd hardly lowered the level more than a couple of swigs, before Fred was calling "Time gentlemen, if you please."

I wasn't too pleased...but what can you say?

Chalky's car was parked outside as well, so he followed me home. I offered him a drink as we went in, but he elected to have a "cuppa, if it was all the same to me."

Mrs. H had left the makings as she always does. So I put the kettle on; then went through the rigmarole of doing the honours.

With the tea poured, we settled back in our armchairs. I fiddled around getting my sugar and milk just right, while Chalky fidgeted. I like to build up suspense.

He broke the silence first. "So what've you got that's so hush bloody hush then? Who's mislaid what?"

"Not mislaid, and it's anything but a what," I said seriously to heighten the drama. "I have a client, with a husband, who has been kidnapped."

He gave a low whistle, and let his eyebrows nudge each other in a frown. After a long thoughtful pause, he said. "I do not like the sound of that Harry. Bit out of your depth, aren't you? I'm not even sure I want to hear about it."

"Oh?…it might be as well," I said. "Tell you what I'll do…sit here and talk to myself. If you happen to pickup the odd word, feel free to comment."

Thinking aloud then, I related the events of the day, with one exception. Naturally, I did the gentlemanly thing by not mentioning why I had been given the bum's rush by Grace.

Chalky made no comments, although I knew he was listening with ill concealed interest; and he heard me out.

I must admit, even though I slanted the tale in my favour, I didn't come out of it looking too good. I was tempted to ask, as I finished the tale, if he had any opinions, but thought better of it. I waited instead.

Clearing his throat, he said, "You took the number of the Morris?"

I nodded.

"Bloody waste of time I expect." he offered, "bound to have been nicked. If they knew you had the diamonds and were waiting for instructions, why the hell would they risk showing themselves by trying to waylay you? None of that makes sense."

"My sentiments exactly, give it some thought then; can you think of a reason?"

Absentmindedly poking at his ear with a finger, and checking it for wax as he pondered, he murmured, "I can think of several." Retrieving his probing finger, to make a clenched fist, he popped it out again and held it up as a counting digit. "One," he counted. "They may not even have the victim, any positive evidence that they have?"

I shook my head.

The next finger leapt erect. "The poor sod is already dead, and I

43

would have to say that is a strong possibility." Another finger came up, "They're able to be complacent because they have the victim in Canada, but want paying here in England." Then, displaying his open hand, "They are plain bloody stupid, somebody is pulling your leg, or you are trying to pull mine?"

I smiled, "All right, let's go for finger three. What set of circumstances would make it desirable to kidnap in one country, and try to collect in another?"

"Well now,"...he took some time idly slurping his tea. "It's unusual, could be a first for all I know. But then, stop and think about that, maybe there is some sense to it. The one thing a kidnapper is banking on is that the family don't go to the police. Devious people policemen are, and villains know it. Then, from the point of view of the family, they know that police intervention doesn't always work. So put yourself in their position, how much confidence would you have, if it meant calling in a foreign police force?"

"Not a lot," I agreed. "I think you have good point Chalky."

"Do you? Well, what about this one? I think you've made a proper balls-up of this case. Let me explain the ground rules of kidnapping. You pay your money then you take your chances about getting the victim back safely. So, think about that Morris you clobbered? Couldn't they have been tailing you, just bidding your time waiting for the right place to flag you down or something? Then they would have demanded the ransom. The bloke was hooded you said, I don't suppose he just happened to have it in his bloody pocket. Any messenger, barring you, would have paid the ransom price and hoped for the best."

"He never asked, you know," I argued defensively.

"I don't expect he did. You run him down with that damned tank you call a car then kick him in the head. I wouldn't be surprised if the poor bugger hadn't forgotten what he wanted to talk to you about?"

All very well for him I thought, while conceding that perhaps he had talked some sense. But then, that is the way he is; always so flaming sensible. It's one thing though, sitting in an armchair swilling tea; it's another ball game to be out there when the fur is flying.

Anyway, hindsight is always better than foresight, as the saying has it. Even if I did agree with most of what he said, and could replay the Morris scene and had done things differently…I was not going to admit it to him. Utter folly to say I had been remiss, unthinking, or a touch hasty. He has a few failings: one of his most irritating is his rotten habit of rubbing things in. No I was not offering him all that ammunition!

I wouldn't stoop to show irritation; but I voiced it. "What's done is flipping well done. Nothing we can do about that now, so let us not dwell, right? The thing we concentrate on now is to anticipate what their next move is likely to be."

"We?" was the dry question, but he said it with an exaggerated shrug to show his supposed resignation. I knew there was no way he could stay out of this one.

That being settled, I pressed on. "I liked your reasoning on why the kidnappers could have planned to snatch Bexley while he was out of the country, then try to collect at this end. So why don't we assume, hypothetically of course, that my astute handling of things so far did thwart their plans. What do you think their next move might be?"

"I think you could well get an obscene phone call telling you how very pissed off they are with you. They might mention too, that if you don't smarten up and mend your ways…you'll get done. That is only hypothetical, of course."

I ignored that petty sarcasm. "You mean they would actually expect me to hand over the stones, without them producing Sir Bexley?"

"Of course they bloody well would. You are being paid to deliver the diamonds, to wherever they tell you. That's it—end of story."

"Not in my book, they don't," I snapped. "They get the ransom the same time I get Bexley; then the story ends. I'm partial to satisfactory conclusions."

"For Pete's sake Harry, I've told you before, you don't think like the rest of us. Doesn't it worry you, that if you don't go along with what they tell you, the poor sod could get snuffed? That's if he hasn't already been."

"Isn't that what I'm saying? Let me ask you this, to clarify my point…would he be in any less danger before I pay, than after? I don't think so. Put it this way, if I convince them that they will only get paid when they produce the victim, the onus will be on them to take very good care of him."

He blew at a passing moth; easily Force 10, surprisingly the moth stayed in the air. "All I can add to what I have already said; is this. When the kidnappers told Lady Bexley to find herself a messenger, you were not what they had in mind. But then I defy any plan to cover a calamity like that. A minor cog Harry; is what you are, or were supposed to be. I'll put money on it though, that you'll gum up the works for them. Their shitty luck, I'd call that!"

I do believe that I detected in Chalky's words the hint of a glimmer of affection. In his own inimical way, I think he just paid me a compliment.

However, without any show of enthusiasm he went on, "Ah, what the hell, might as well give me the number of the Morris, I'll chase it up for you. Anything else I can waste my time on, while I'm at it?"

"Matter of fact there is," I said as I was jotting down the number, "Keep an enquiring eye on Grace Watkins for me. If that wastes your time, at least you'll find her worth looking at."

"I'll scan that lady with a very enquiring eye," he offered. "I imagine it has occurred to you, maybe, that what we have here is an inside job? The kidnappers seem very well informed on movements and business connections. I'm going to take a good hard look at a number of things. I won't waste my breath telling you not to do anything rash, but maybe I can protect you from yourself."

"Now Chalky, don't go stamping those size twelve's of yours about too obviously. Remember; other eyes could be watching you. I'd hate to have to ream you out for making a balls up."

"I don't have your knack for it son."

With which parting shot, he left. Not too bad an exit. I was sure though that I had him well and truly hooked. He would have a good sniff around, and as a bloodhound-he is good.

CHAPTER FIVE

Nothing like a session with Chalky I decided, after seeing him off the premises, to bring a chap down to earth in a hurry.

Although his comments had been helpful in confirming much of what I had already figured out, his criticisms had me reviewing my position as it stood now. Which gave me plenty to get my teeth into.

I poured myself a generous glass of Scotch and made myself comfortable in my armchair. As an aid to achieving the desired atmosphere for meditation, I turned the lights out.

Nature's floodlight, in the shape of an almost full moon, cast its glow through the window behind me, gently highlighting the living room furniture—which didn't look too bad in that light, teasingly reminding me of the soft lights in Grace's flat.

I hoped the incident in the Mucky Duck wouldn't create repercussions for her. The pub was quite close to her place, and she had mentioned that she ate there sometimes. I wondered if the low life in the pub might know where she lived. Well Chalky was going to cast an eye in her direction, which eased my concern quite a lot.

I must have sat there some time, just letting my thoughts float, because I became aware that I had been dozing. Bed was beckoning, so I drained the last of my whisky and started to heave myself out of the chair. Then I heard the crunch of the gravel outside the window.

Not the pebble-skitter of a foraging dog, nor the rhythmic crunch of a visitor on foot. I cocked an ear…sonar on fine tune. Suspiciously I rolled out of the chair; then slowly and silently moved on my hands and knees to the window. As I raised my head, my eye found a peephole in the lace curtain. Nothing that moved registered in my consciousness, as I let my eyes sweep the driveway and the front garden.

Kneeling thus, and beginning to feel like a Peeping Tom, I mentally scolded myself for indulging in such childish behaviour.

But, being the cautious type that I am, I watched a little longer— still nothing moved.

Ah, I decided, it wouldn't be the first time one of Ted Bailey's cows had done a number on my flower beds…but surely not at night.

"Don't move a muscle Potts," said a voice from behind me. "Just stay where you are; put your hands flat on the floor."

Wasn't hard to figure out who that was, I recognised the voice.

The next communication from him was his boot up my arse; a message of considerable impact. I'd like to say that the blow to my pride hurt more…but it didn't.

"That's a token of what I owe you, you stupid bastard," he hissed unnecessarily.

Totally occupied as I was with clenching my teeth, I declined to argue the point. I'm sure, at that moment in time, had I been able to form words, I would not have been able to think of a reply that would have done me credit.

"Get up, you self opinionated slime-bag, get your backside in that chair before I'm tempted to repeat the treatment."

The sound of his voice moved away from me. I chanced a glance over my shoulder and saw the vague outline of his figure. He was standing across the room from me, the moonlight reflecting a metallic glitter from his outstretched hand.

"Yes it's a gun," he confirmed. "And you'd be doing me a favour if you make me use it."

I took his word, and decided not to do him any favours. I turned round slowly to face him; then lowered myself very gently into the chair.

"Now isn't this cosy," he drooled.

If he was looking for confirmation from me, it would have been in the negative, so I buttoned my lip.

"Not as eloquent now? You lippy freak of nature. All that verbal diarrhoea you farted out, what are you…a mental retard?"

I wasn't going to answer that either.

"Tell me…Piss-pot. Weren't you engaged to deliver a consignment of diamonds?"

Well that one was worth a reply. "No, I was hired to affect an exchange."

"Exactly right chum, let me spell it out for you. You hand over the diamonds right now. In exchange for which, I give you the location of where you can collect the old codger."

"Not good enough," I chanced. "As I told you earlier; produce Sir Bexley and you've got yourself a deal."

"I've got myself a deal," he crowed, waving the gun. "This is your ticket to a box, or life, take your pick."

I shook my head, then in case he couldn't see it; said "No"

"What d'you mean, no…you ready for a box then?"

"It's not that," I spit out fast, just in case his finger was itchy. "It's just that it is not a good idea, for either one of us. I'd be dead, and you'd be up the creek; without the diamonds."

"You mean you've hidden them or something," he said as my words sunk in.

"What do you think? I'm not that mentally deficient. You hid Bexley; I hid the ransom."

That had him thinking, but not for long. "So I shoot one of your kneecaps off, the other one too if you don't come across fast. For what," he coaxed. "She can't be paying you that much!"

"A pittance," I agreed. "You could always try me with a better offer."

"So that's the way the wind blows is it. OK, now we're getting somewhere, looking for a bigger slice of the pie are we?"

"It's a big pie," I reminded him. "It looks even bigger now I'm holding it."

"Tell you what," he said, "and only so we can get this over with quick. Take three diamonds for yourself, and give me the rest. You'll be getting something like fifteen thousand quids worth. Not something you make everyday, so let's get on with it."

More the pity I thought, as I hesitated long enough to pander to decency before I grabbed his offer. "Sounds good, I agreed. "An offer, that smacks of a sharp mind." A little flattery never goes amiss. "Could work out well for both of us...I will then become an accomplice so you can stop worrying about me being able to identify you. I shall be suitably compensated for lowering my ethical standards, and you get advance delivery of the ransom. I like it. A sound business arrangement...we both profit."

"Right, it's a deal then."

"Right you are. Tell you what...I'll give you an even better deal. How would it be if you took all of the diamonds; you know what to do with them, I'd rather have cash, even less, say ten thousand."

"Like hell you will," he snapped. "That's a delaying tactic, you now damned well I haven't got that kind of money in my pocket. Shut you face, and get the sodding diamonds..."

I quickly interrupted, still concerned about my kneecaps, "I don't have the diamonds in my pocket either, you see. So, you go and get the money and I'll get the diamonds when you aren't looking. Then we can meet cordially in a public place, where we will consummate our deal."

He mulled that over—looking for ways to shaft me no doubt; then he seemed to come to a decision. "All right, I'll meet you later today."

"That would be too soon, I told you, you wouldn't find the diamonds, they aren't here. Beyond my control I'm afraid, but I wasn't expecting this get-together so soon, was I"

"Shit," he swore, and I felt the spray of spittle from the end of the word. "You're pressing your bloody luck Potts."

"I'm truly sorry about it, but it did seem like a good idea to salt the ransom away; big responsibility to have them laying around. How was I to even guess that we might become business associates? The earliest I can get them to you would be early tomorrow, which, as it's now already Saturday, would be Sunday."

"I know what day it is moron; where on Sunday?"

"Where would be a good place for you? I asked. "I have no wish to cause you any more trouble now, let's make this an amicable relationship, eh."

"London, would suit me."

"London it is then. How about, in front of Buckingham Palace? Let's make it, say, at eleven in the morning. The Guards will be doing their stuff then…we can get lost in the crowd."

"It'll do, that's public enough. But I give you fair warning Potts, no buggering about. I'll take a good look at those stones, and they had better be right! One more false step from you and Bexley goes into the history book, so keep that thought in your head."

"Speaking of whom," I reminded him, "I still insist on some proof of his being alive. Nothing gruesome like an ear or a finger…that would constitute damaged goods. You'll understand that I would like to come out of this assignment, smelling like a rose."

"Be grateful you're coming out of it, not smelling like a corpse. You'll have to take my word that the old man is presently in good shape. You guessed I suppose that we don't have him in England? So I can't give you proof."

It was my turn to mull things over. "A simple taped message would be OK," I suggested. "Over the telephone would be fine. See if you can get it to me by seven on Sunday morning, I'll have to leave at about that time to get to London for eleven"

This produced another pregnant pause. Finally, "All right, I might be able to arrange that, but I'm having second thoughts about the meeting place. It's a bit too public, I want to examine the diamonds very closely, and up against the railings at Buck House will be a bit tricky."

"I don't see why. We could do it this way," I suggested. I'll hollow out a book and put the diamonds in it. Then if you have to use one of

51

those jeweller's gizmos to do your inspection-well you'll just look like a short sighted reader. You could do much the same. Put the money between the covers of a pocket book, a thick one, five hundred £20 notes equals a good read. I can count the pages...while you appraise."

"Smart arse, maybe I should smack you across the mouth with this pistol, just to see if you have a sense of humour about a toothless grin. You have a devious mind Potts, not much sense, but you're tricky with it. I won't trust you for a second, don't ever forget it. Twice you got lucky with me." As he was speaking he began to back out towards the door with the gun still pointing at me. "It won't happen again. Now, when I go through this door we'll meet once more, on Sunday. I will keep my side of the bargain, and by Christ you'd better keep yours. From then on, start watching your back. I hate your guts, you arrogant bastard...I'll snuff you out yet."

With which, he backed through the door and was gone.

I stayed where I was, still in the chair.

In my line of business it is not unusual to be threatened, by thoroughly irritated people. One does even get used to it. So I don't get all of a quiver, or often take offence. But this chap's parting shots, I found disturbing. He hadn't blustered; he'd quietly and simply stated a fact.

I gave him time to get off my property, then got up and refilled my glass.

It's quite an exhausting business, verbally manipulating a nutter with a gun. Quick thinking is required. From his initial intention to kill me, which I'm sure he would have if I had given him the diamonds, to merely the loss of my kneecaps, was in itself a dodgy operation.

The thing giving me the most trouble, in the stress department, was the fact that the diamonds were still in my jacket pocket...and I was still wearing it.

I wearily toddled off to bed, and drifted off to sleep wondering if I would have handed them over before or after my first kneecap popped off.

The last thing I remember thinking...was that I still had the diamonds and I'd won some time. Time for what, escaped me.

CHAPTER SIX

The following morning, after a late breakfast prepared by Mrs. H, I decided to visit Chalky.

I had made an effort to reach him by telephone shortly after I got out of bed, but my attempts were thwarted by a succession of busy signals. I presumed he was doing his legwork the easy way; with his dialling finger. But then the smell of breakfast cooking had proven more tempting than my urge to use the phone.

Fair to say; I seldom allow business matters to hurry me through one of Mrs. H's servings. She is an artist. I have never had that traditional fare looking or tasting any better than one of hers. A few slices of fried tomatoes together with half a pound of fried mushrooms, as a garnish on a foundation of fried bread, making the perfect base to support the bacon and eggs. The whole delectable creation washed down by buckets of tea. Occasionally one gets a bonus when Mrs. H doesn't hang about chatting, as was the case this morning. Then, with the morning paper propped up against the teapot this delicious meal is devoured by a happy face being entertained by the antics of the politicians.

Which is why, most of my morning was in the past tense before I rapped on the door of Chalky's garage-cum-workshop.

A token rap before I opened the door and walked in; he was still on the telephone. An eyebrow gave me a wriggle as he turned to see who it was. Whoever he was talking to had his full attention…the big chap's pencil was at work.

I passed the time by wandering around the workshop trying to assess the progress on his little steam engine. The locomotive's chassis was propped up with its wheels clear of the bench, displaying an intricate assortment of rods, cams, and levers.

I stood at the bench trying to work out what did what to what. Just as I thought I had it figured the "uh-uh's" ceased.

"Thanks Frank, I'm obliged," preceded the clonk of the phone going down on its cradle.

"Jackpot," Chalky swivelled his chair in my direction and treated me to a satisfied smirk.

"So what have you won?" I teased.

"Did a run down on the Morris," he said, ignoring my quip. "Don't know how you get so lucky. If you dropped down a sewer, you'd climb out covered in chocolate. I'd have laid odds on that car being stolen.

"Ah," I offered.

"Right, want to hear more?"

"I'm all ears."

"You can say that again," he scored, "It's what's between them I wonder about."

"A mind like a razor," I claimed, "and it's all agog, so tell me all mate."

He raised his notebook. "Shut your mouth then and listen." He started to read aloud. "Aforementioned vehicle; subject of accident report which states, that the other vehicle left the scene. Other vehicle is described as a large green coloured car, maybe a Rover, no number plate seen." Looking up from his notes; "Got the colour right, left some paint there did you?"

"None of mine, the Chalky White special worked a treat."

"I designed that bumper to protect you from a rear-ender. I still think that petrol tank on the arse-end of a Bentley is lethal. But, if I'd known that you were going to use it as a battering ram, I could have welded some spikes on it."

"Works fine the way it is," I offered.

"Tested and passed then?"

"No question. Wonder why they filed an accident report?"

"Because," he said dryly, "the bloody driver was carted off to hospital, so what else could they do? But you'll notice they didn't give any information which would lead the police to you."

"I noticed. Was the driver damaged much?"

"No, but no thanks to you I'm sure. Concussion and contusions; he's still in hospital. Under observation…medical that is. Name of…" glancing at his notes, " one Rowland Cooke, with an e."

"Well I cooked his goose didn't I," I couldn't resist that, but it didn't get any appreciation from Chalky—unless a sigh, a snort and a loosening of phlegm count as some recognition. Anyway I stuck to business by asking, "And who does the report name as the passenger?"

"Peter Hepworth," he said, "and let's hear you play around with that."

Wouldn't dare," I confessed, "more than my life's worth." Fortunately that one passed him by.

Or did it…"Quite right," was what he said, which was nicely ambiguous. "There you have it," he went on, "not bad for a mornings work eh?"

"Not too shabby at all," I agreed. I should have been a touch more gushing in my congratulations, but another of his failings is an inclination to get a swelled head when praise is tossed in his direction, a condition which suits so few of us, so I bit my tongue. "Useless information though," I reminded him. "We can't use it can we?"

"I suppose not," he said reluctantly, shaking his head, "which is a great pity. It's worth sweet Fanny Adams though, until they release the victim. Be a different story then. I'll have them in the pokey so fast it'll make their bloody heads spin."

"Do you think so Chalky? We might know who did it, but I have my doubts; that with what we've got on them, we could prove a thing."

He stood up, and thrust both hands into his trouser pockets as he lumbered along the workbench in a preoccupied manner.

Then he turned to me and summed it up concisely. "Ah, shit."

"Never mind old son," I comforted. "As you pointed out, so pointedly, I'm just the messenger. It's not your job to apprehend the villains."

"Be nice though," he ruminated. Then he looked at me and appeared to perk up. "Well now,' he smiled, "if you've finally got that through your thick skull, there's some hope for you, not to mention the victim. With all the fart-arsing-about you've done so far, the only villain likely to be charged is you...for hit-and-run."

Time to change the subject; so I did, "Want to give me a demonstration of all these bits and pieces?" I asked, indicating his locomotive parts. "You say it runs on air? So let's see it."

The self satisfied smirk he'd been levelling at me dissolved into a grin, "Thought you'd never ask!"

He moved over to where his pride and joy was sitting up on its chocks, grabbing an oilcan on his way. He shot a couple of squirts of oil down a copper pipe that was sticking up in front of the contraption. "Lubricating the cylinders," he explained. Then taking an air hose, which was connected to a compressor, he snapped it on the pipe he'd just given a shot of oil. "Now watch this," he commanded like a conjurer about to produce a rabbit.

I did, I watched as he put a finger on a miniature lever situated at the rear of the chassis—he has quite a flair for the dramatic, gently, he eased the lever forward...but nothing was happening. I began to think we were heading for something of an anti-climax. But then, there was the faintest hiss of air and the bits started to move. Things began to move to and fro and around, the eccentrics bobbed up and down; the wheels started to turn. Moving in unison with a slow smooth rhythm, slow enough for me to be able to see as I watched in fascination, just what did move what. I could understand Chalky's pride in having made such a slick piece of machinery and his joyful enthusiasm in seeing it actually worked. I caught some of it myself.

I felt he had every right to get big-headed about it, so I offered my congratulations with such out of character enthusiasm that the poor old lad looked almost embarrassed.

Not something he is used to, being embarrassed; I helped him out by asking. "What was it that got you so interested in model trains?"

He thought about that a while, "Underprivileged childhood, I expect." The time he took in arriving at that conclusion washed some of the red out of his face. "I remember," he went on, "looking at the wind-up kind when I was a kid, they hadn't come up with the electric ones then. Every Christmas the shop windows were full of them, and every Christmas I was disappointed. There was one in particular that I remember, a smaller version of this one I'm building, I wanted that one so bad I could almost taste it. But once again, it was…no dice. Ah well," he said with a shrug, "don't suppose that did me any harm in the long run. Certainly made me value the things I did get."

"And it doesn't look like you're short of anything now," I remarked as I swung my eyes around the workshop.

"Always one more thing though isn't there," he said. "Fact of life," he added with a chuckle.

"So what's your one more thing?"

"A milling machine, when I can afford it. I would like to put flutes in these connecting and coupling rods…can't do that on a lathe."

"Everything in time eh," I offered. "Speaking of which, why don't we slide along to the Rose for a pie and a pint? That is, unless you want to nip off, to put your mind at rest regarding Miss Grace Watkins?"

"I've got time for that later," he said. "Time for lunch anyway—as you are buying. Suppose you fancy her, this Miss Watkins? So what else is new, eh?"

I shrugged nonchalantly, "Wouldn't want her to come to any harm over that fiasco in the Dirty Duck. I know you suggested last night, or at least inferred that this might be an inside job…and Grace is on the inside, but I don't think she is in any way involved."

"There you go again Harry," he snorted. "You just finished

admitting that you're just the bleeding messenger. Why don't you leave it at that? Why keep poking around? I'll tell you another thing, while I've got my mouth going. You're as smart as they come about most things, but not about women. You're as daft as a brush when it comes to them. You go around picking up birds like there's no tomorrow. Believe anything they tell you; you will. Blinded by their bloody knickers, you are son."

He was quite breathless after that outburst. I treated him to my sheepish grin.

"Ah come on; buy me lunch," he said shaking his head and flapping a hand down in a "what's the use" gesture. "Then I'll go and give the girl the once over. No use talking to you. I offer you the wisdom of my years, and it runs off you like water off a duck's back. Or does it? I'm never sure. You're a crafty young bugger."

If only he knew…what I knew.

I bought him his lunch, during which I managed to keep things to generalities. Cricket, roses, and dogs. Fred the landlord related some amusing stories about dogs. He and his wife own several greyhounds, and race them. Judging by the tales he told about their occasional winners, I formed the opinion that the thrill they experienced in the Winners Circle, equalled that of the Royals when they do the same thing, when they get lucky with their horses.

Eventually Chalky made like he was about ready to leave, so I thought it was time to ask him something without telling him much.

"Before you head off," I asked him, "how would you like to accompany me and see the Changing of the Guards at Buckingham Palace tomorrow?"

He eyeballed me with what must be as close to a "stunned" look as he was capable of, "Lost your marbles have you?"

"Probably," I conceded, "I'd like you to be dressed like a tourist too, and have a camera slung around your neck."

"What the hell for?"

"I can't tell you what for, all I'm asking is, can you?"

"Harry," he said, his stunned look going into the stiffed-lipped mode. "You're asking a lot of an ex London Bobby. Me, a bloody rubberneck, what if one of the lads on that beat saw me. You'd better give me a sodding good reason!"

"I'd better not," I advised him. "I have one, a good reason, but I'm not going to give it to you. Because, one, you wouldn't want to know, and two, I don't need a lecture right now on the ethics of investigative behaviour."

"You could be right about one, so don't bother telling me. About two, a lecture on your behaviour would be like farting up-wind—the folly of which even you might work out. See you at the Palace? Just don't stand down wind of me! I'm a patient man, with a lot of self restraint, but I'm about due to blow."

I nodded, "Yes, I'll see you at the palace…up-wind…you make your own way there."

The few qualms I harboured regarding my keeping quiet about the visit of the kidnapper, I easily quashed. My arrangement with Peter Hepworth, as I now knew him to be, could not be revealed to Chalky. He does at times, obligingly turn a blind eye to my many meanderings off the path of accepted police methods, but the merest hint of my acceptance of a bribe, however deviously manoeuvred, could well have him teetering on the edge of apoplexy.

No amount of plausible explanations on my part, would give him solace, or me redemption.

This was clearly a time, I reasoned, to activate the need to know format. Which summed up, means…don't tell Chalky.

Anyway, visions of recapturing the kudos of the publicity that surrounded the Finchly Affair were still flitting temptingly through my imagination. If there is one thing I have picked up in this investigative business, it is the value of publicity. Who would have heard of Sherlock Holmes, without the exposure provided by Dr. Watson? I'm not saying the old sleuth wasn't on the ball, but, if nobody knew about it, what good was it?

Of course Chalky, not being a Watson, wouldn't reason that out. No, not for me, the mundane steps of a messenger…star billing every time!

So I made a phone call to Lady Bexley, who reported no word from the abductors; which hardly surprised me at all. Naturally I contributed the required selection of comforting phrases to boost her moral, although it sounded as though it was standing up quite well. I hung up after offering my belief that the waiting would end soon. Needless to say, my tongue was in my cheek—quite comfortably. Out of necessity over the years, it has fashioned a familiar niche there.

CHAPTER SEVEN

The thundering bell on my alarm clock vibrating the top of my bedside table sucked me out of unconsciousness. My mind went on a search, of who I was, where I was, and what was urgent.

The only out of the ordinary item, my half awake mind could latch onto was…an imminent incoming phone call. 'Seven in the morning' had been my instruction to Hepworth, and I saw it was six in the morning now.

Time will tell, I determined, as I crawled out of bed and slithered into the shower. An examination of my backside in the mirror (a depressing eye opener) as I gingerly dried off, revealed one hell of a bruise. The sight had my hate buds smacking their lips, waiting for the elected target of their wrath. Peter (Snotnose) Hepworth was going to get it; one way or another…both ways if I could manage it!

The bruise told me it wasn't going to be a joyride getting up to London on my motorcycle. But then, I reminded myself, the road to fame and fortune in the finding game is seldom smooth. My arse, like the rest of my parts, must learn to turn the other cheek.

One of the reasons I was using a bike today was so that I would be more mobile, another reason was that I could wear bulky clothing and a helmet without looking conspicuous. I had things to conceal on my person, a tape recorder for example. I know MI5 have gadgets small enough to fit in a button, but they are not too readily available in the real world. The tinted face shield on the helmet would hide my face, not that it is that ugly, but it is often a help to travel incognito. I was hoping that Chalky would get a photo of Hepworth; but I had no desire to have a picture of me consorting with the criminal element.

However, I was up and alert, and downing my second cup of coffee when the phone rang.

I picked it up, to be questioned by a voice saying "Hairy Parts?" Which gave me an instant clue; I was listening to a North American accent.

"Speaking," I replied.

"Got a message for you," the voice went on. A click or two, a pause, then an unmistakably English voice said, "This is Sir Aubrey Bexley. I am advising you that I am in good health. I confirm that I am indeed being shown a newspaper dated the twenty second of July. You have permission to comply with the arrangements for my safe release."

After another series of clicks, the original voice said, "Got that?"

"There is…" I started to say before the line went dead. So I presumed that whatever I was likely to get, I had got. I rewound the tape in the recorder and pressed the play button to check that I had got it.

I rewound the tape again, then dialled Lady Bexley's number.

"Hello," said a sleepy voiced Lady.

"Good-morning Lady Bexley," I said. "I'd just like you to listen to this, it should cheer you up."

Holding the recorder against the mouthpiece, I switched it on.

After it had played through I lifted the phone back to my ear. I heard muffled sobs and gave her a few moments before asking, "Are you all right?"

Which is often a bloody stupid question, but what else can you say? Especially with women, who cry for joy, as well as sorrow, so there wasn't much to do then, but eavesdrop while she struggled with her emotions…resolving as I listened, to inflict some grievous bodily harm to Hepworth at his soonest inconvenience.

"I'm all right now Harry," Lady Bexley eventually reported. "It was such a shock, but so wonderful and so terribly moving to hear Aubrey's voice and know he was well."

"No doubt, about it being his voice then?" I asked.

"None whatever…not the least doubt, is it going to be all right now Harry?"

"I'm sure it will be. Try to relax now, no need to sit by the phone, let me handle things from here on will you?"

"Oh of course, how on earth did you manage to get them to contact you," she asked excitedly.

"Nasty story," I said, putting a touch of drama in the tone, "best not repeated."

"I see," she said. "How long do you think Harry, before my husband is released?"

"That's a tough one," I replied. "I'm not calling the shots in the time department, but I'd say about three days could see an end to it."

This about wrapped up the call, so after the usual formalities I rang off.

Shortly after that, suitably attired, I was ready for my trip to London. My tape recorder loaded with fresh tape was zipped down in one thigh pocket. The diamonds, nestling in cotton wool in the prepared cavity of a book, were safely battened down in the other one. I was overdressed; couldn't be helped, but I was going to be hot in London.

As I went out of my back door, Mrs. H was bustling along the path towards me at a great rate.

"Morning Mr. Potts, are you coming or going?"

"Morning Mrs. H…going."

"What about your breakfast?"

"Pushed for time; I'll grab something later."

"Not good for you to be riding them bikes of yours, without a proper breakfast in your stomach," she grumbled. "And mark my words you'll get nothing but rubbish in one of them cafe places."

I couldn't argue about the latter, but sensing her feelings were hurt; I leaned down and gave her a kiss on the cheek. "Sorry Mrs. H, but I really do have to go."

"Oh, get on with you," she said, showing a cute little blush.

She scuttled off towards the hen coop; and I unlocked the door of the stable.

The horses I keep in my stable are not of the four legged variety, they are the two-wheeled version of a mount…motor cycles. They are as much a hobby to me, as locomotives are to Chalky. Maybe at times I am just as garrulous as he about my interest, though I doubt that.

I can go back to 1940, when I got my first motorbike. It was a 1932 BSA 350cc Sloper, I swapped a piano accordion for it. My mother had visions of me being a pianist. Probably because I had learned to play When I Grow to Old to Dream with one finger (mother loved that song) and she also had a soft spot for the piano accordion, so I got to play her tune with one finger on that. It did help actually…you can hold the note longer than on a piano, so the left hand isn't missed as much. Anyway, I ran into a lad who had this BSA bike and thought the piano accordion was his passport to fame and fortune. He set off on foot.

I was 18 years old at that time. The war was underway, the evacuation of Dunkirk had taken place, and the Battle of Britain was heating up. Air raids were a nightly affair so I decided enough was enough and off I went to the Recruiting Office to join the RAF. My first choice was to hop into a Spitfire and bag myself a few dozen German bombers, so the Flight Sergeant in attendance suggested that I should go to London and present my case before a Selection Board. A free train ride to London wasn't to be sniffed at, so a couple of days later I was putting my case to a bunch of elderly RAF officers. They decided not to trust me with a Spitfire, but offered me a position in a bomber's gun turret, that was if I could learn how to tap out the Morse code on a radio. That sounded like a lot of fun; then I could pop over to Germany and drop some bombs on them…pay back time. So I signed up for the duration.

The Morse code proved to be more difficult than it seemed, and as I had mentioned my expertise on a motor bike, it was decided that General Montgomery could use me to ride about, delivering RAF dispatches in the Western Desert. So off I went, just in time for El Alemein.

What a wonderful war I had, being paid to do what I liked doing most…riding motorcycles, and every time I broke one or wore it out, I got a new one. I rode them everywhere: round the Pyramids, up and down the Western Desert—until Rommel packed it in. Tobruk, Benghazi, mostly escorting convoys…no mean chore riding herd on a few miles of lorries and trying to keep them together. Through and around Palestine, Syria, Iraq, Iran, Baghdad, Basra, Bahrain, and once, even under a camel's belly (another story). In Winston Churchill's immortal words: "Never before in the field of human conflict, has so much been owed to so few." He was of course referring to Dispatch Riders

Well perhaps I can be as garrulous as Chalky, I thought, as I swung open the doors of the stable.

I have two bikes. One is a Vincent, a classic, and they haven't made those for a while. The other is a 500cc Norton 16H. This is the model that I spent most of my time on during those RAF days. This one I picked up at a surplus sale, and restored.

I whipped the dust sheet off the Norton. It was to be my mount for the day; inconspicuous but plenty big enough, to thread a way through the streets of London.

Throwing a leg over her, I gingerly tested my tender portions, bearable—but only just.

Turn the petrol on then a tickle on the carburettor; valve lifter up and a stamp on the kick-start. Then a slight turn on the twist grip and she burst into the familiar rumble. I pulled my helmet on, and buttoned up while the exhaust note settled down to a healthy beat; then I was away.

I decided to stay on the back roads as I headed off in the direction of London, their curves and undulations are much more interesting to a motorcyclist. Just a nice quiet Sunday outing, as far as Lewisham, then I joined the clog-up as I made my way along the Old Kent Road. Not too bad, with it being Sunday, but still pretty hot and smokey.

Certainly no one had followed me today; the cross country route I had taken had made that impossible, without my being aware of it. But then, why should they follow me? They knew where I was going, at least one of them did.

After jack-rabbiting in the traffic up to, and over the Vauxhall Bridge, I checked the time. It was an hour and a half before the Guards did their thing at the Palace…I was right on schedule.

Turning right onto Rochester Row, I nipped along Whitehall and left the bike on its stand in front of Charing Cross Station. Riding a bike in the city has many advantages, one of them being the ease of parking.

Swinging my helmet by its chin-strap I walked into the Charing Cross Hotel; the hotel at the entrance to the station. A visit to the public lavatories enabled me to shed my riding gear, and subsequently make my way into the hotel restaurant, with some degree of decorum.

The breakfast crowds had thinned out so I had no problem spotting Chalky. He was sitting at a table peering at me over the top of a newspaper.

"Sorry to be late," I remarked conversationally as I arrived at his table.

"How the hell can you be late? I didn't even know you were coming." He lowered his paper slightly as he spoke. He did not look happy.

Ignoring his lack of welcome, I dumped my helmet and gear on a vacant chair and seated myself at the table opposite him.

His paper was back up in front of his face, but I enquired anyway, "Eaten yet?"

"Thank you for your concern, "he said sarcastically, "but yes, I have." He was definitely miffed.

"Do you mind?" I asked, rapping on the table until the paper came down, then I gestured at the empty table in front of me.

"Please yourself," he replied, and up went the paper again. I had been dismissed.

Managing to catch the eye of one of a pair of waitresses who were pantomiming the batting of imaginary crumbs from an already spotless table while engaging in a totally absorbing chat, I gave her what I felt was an engaging wink. Obviously it was not entirely magnetic, for I had to wait until she delivered what was apparently the punch line before she sidled over to our table.

"Large pot of tea, bacon and eggs and an orange juice, in any order…as long as it's fast," I said, smiling at her.

"Right away sir."

As she walked away, Chalky slapped his paper together, "Fifteen bloody minutes I sat here, before I got any service," he grumbled sulkily.

"What do you expect, the way you're dressed? She thought you were a tourist."

"Ha, bloody ha. In case you haven't twigged; I'm a bit pissed off with you son. Just what the hell are you up to? You make me nervous. I'm offering my help, and you haven't got the bloody decency to tell me what's going on."

"I know, and don't think I'm not sorry, and I'm not blaming you for being cranky," I said as humbly as I am capable of. "But, I couldn't dream of involving you in anything shady, and what I am up to as you put it, could definitely be construed as that. Better you don't know…you'd worry."

He occupied himself for a while in folding his paper, "OK, enough said. Change of subject. How did you know I would be in here for my breakfast?"

"Lucky guess," I offered as I thanked the waitress who had arrived with the pot of tea. Picking it up, I asked by a gesture with the pot, if Chalky wanted a top-up. He answered by pushing his cup under the poised spout. As I poured I went on, "You stayed at this hotel on your honeymoon; you told me once that you pop in here for breakfast when you're up this way."

"Remarkable memory you have," he murmured absentmindedly; his thoughts I surmised, being in the past.

67

I had demolished a goodly portion of my bacon and eggs, before he surfaced again.

"You know, I've just been working it out," he smirked, "it's going to cost you as much for our breakfasts as it cost me and Milly to spend the night here. Prices have gone up a bit in thirty years."

"Cheeky bugger," I said, wiping my mouth with a napkin as I thankfully realised we were back on an even keel. I carried on, "How did you make out in Tunbridge Wells?"

"No problem there. I dropped into the Swan and talked to the landlord. The snot-rags were not locals, so you don't have to worry about Miss Watkins, leastwise not on that count. I reserve judgement on other counts though...you and the ladies, I don't know Harry!"

"Incidentally," he grinned, "you could become a legend in that pub. The landlord gave me a step by step account of your nifty footwork. Said he'd never seen anything like it. Made me quite sorry I missed it."

"You know how these tales get exaggerated," I suggested. "They grow with the telling, anyway you know I play a good game of football...I see a ball, I just have to boot it."

That turned the subject around to the football scene, and the current deplorable state of that art.

Chalky finally consulted his watch, made some pointed remarks, no doubt looking for sympathy about how long it was going to take him to walk up the Mall to the Palace, then left when he didn't get any reaction from me.

I drained the pot of tea and chatted up the waitresses before paying the bill and leaving. He was right about the cost factor.

St. James' Park looked splendid in the sunshine as I tooled my bike up the Mall; circled Queen Victoria's statue and pulled into the curb on the corner of Constitution Hill.

It was still half an hour before the Guard's changed, and already there were a good sprinkling of tourists—judging by the complexions and the cameras. Most of them were lined up in front of the Palace; snapping pictures through the iron railings.

Putting the bike on the stand I pulled a street map out of my pocket and opened it on the petrol tank, in an endeavour to blend into the general scene.

Casting an eye about me I wondered if I would be able to pick Hepworth out, and decided that I shouldn't have too much trouble…I'd had a good look at him when I bent the Morris, fairly stocky sort of chap about my age, perhaps a bit older, light brown hair hazel eyes and clean-shaven. with a strong looking chin and wide cheekbones. An athletic type I'd say, although I'm not sure where I got that impression, because the only time I had a look at his body motion, was while he was on his hands and knees.

He'd know me all right, but not unless I took my helmet off, which was not in my plans.

Letting my eyes browse through the crowd, and letting them skip quickly past the female, black, and Oriental faces, I concluded that Hepworth was not present.

Chalky was…I spotted him. He'd overdone the tourist guise a bit, he looked like a visitor from another era…he was sporting a Panama hat.

Prompted by idle interest in his hat, I started to scrutinise other assorted headgear. Amazing what people will perch on their heads, but Hepworth's face wasn't under any of them.

Then a taxi pulled into the curb just ahead of me, a single passenger alighted and as he turned to pay the driver I saw my target had arrived. Peter Hepworth, decked out in a blue track-suit, wearing white running shoes and carrying a small sports bag.

I watched as he walked towards the palace railings, sparing no more than a glance at the Palace, then turning his back on it and gazing around to peruse the spectators. His scrutiny included me and went on without any hesitation.

He stayed facing the crowd, his eyes panning over it. I sat on the bike, trying to look casual by occasionally studying the street map, while watching the crowd thicken. When I felt it was dense enough to make individual movement less noticeable, I folded the map, dismounted, and stood up.

Switching the tape recorder on, I cast an eye in Chalky's direction and noted that he was watching me. I gave him a nod of my helmet, then homed in on Hepworth, not exactly in a straight line. I had to work my way through the growing crowd until I was standing alongside him. He still made no sign of recognition, although we were by this time almost face to helmet. He was still concentrating his attention on the crowd about him, presumably trying to locate me.

"Impressive, isn't it?" I murmured almost in his ear. "Daily event, yet seldom fails to attract a crowd like this." Enough words, I felt, for him to identify me, unless he was dimmer than I thought.

He looked at me warily, as though his brain might be getting into gear. Then leaning closer, he questioned, "Potts?"

"None other," I agreed. "Weren't expecting anyone else were you?"

"No, and there'd better not be." Then looking pointedly at my attire, he added "What's with the clowns outfit?"

"I'm bashful," I said, watching Chalky busy with his camera. "Come on," I went on, "it's a bit crowded here. Over by my bike, we can talk there."

I moved…he followed. Once out of the crowd, he asked, "You bring the diamonds?"

"Yes," I said, "I received the message from Sir Bexley, confirming that he is all right. That was all I asked; I'm satisfied."

"I'm so glad," he said sarcastically. "So, show them to me."

Unzipping my pocket I pulled out the book and lifted the cover, giving him a glimpse of the gems nestled in the black velvet lined cavity. Then I quickly snapped the cover shut again. "I trust you have an equally interesting book?"

He shook his sports bag, by way of an answer. "I told you I wanted a good look at those stones; this place isn't private enough." He looked towards the Mall, "Over there, in the park, away from this mob."

"All right, but I can't leave my bike here unattended. I'll ride it over and park it by the public conveniences across from Clarence House. I'll wait for you in the park, should be quiet enough there."

He nodded curtly, and strutted off.

Throwing a leg over the bike, I made a production of digging in pockets, while I looked for Chalky's whereabouts. I located him and saw he was paying attention. When he saw me looking in his direction, he sauntered towards me, still playing the tourist with his camera.

He came close, turned his back on me, and said softly out of the side of his mouth, "I got some good ones, I hope. Full face, and profile."

"I'm meeting him across in St. James' Park," I said from inside the helmet. "But, I can manage fine now. I'll meet you back at Charing Cross…in an hour or so."

Kicking the bike into life, I blipped the throttle a couple of times to clear a path through the crowd, and moved off just as the Guards came marching round the corner to add their colour and drums and bugles to the scene.

Parking in the shallow lay-by, just at the entrance to the park, I walked carrying my helmet now, roughly halfway along the footpath leading towards the lake. There, I settled myself down on the grass in the centre of an unoccupied area, and waited for the approach of Mr. Bloody Hepworth.

I did not have to wait long…he was jogging. I got to my feet just before he reached me.

"Right! Let's trade," he said without preamble, and reached into his bag.

I moved closer to him, anything other than a book coming out of his bag and he'd find himself on his arse in a considerable hurry.

He produced a book, which he held out towards me, then made a couple of upward gestures with it.

I gathered he was telling me to cough up, so I pulled my book out, and we suspiciously traded…four hands occupied simultaneously.

He stepped back a few paces, knelt down on the grass, and made like a jeweller.

I counted the money. Thumbing through incoming funds always gives me an exquisite feeling of well being, and it took great control over my facial muscles to hide a smug smile…but I managed.

His endeavours appeared to satisfy him also, his facial control wasn't up to mine; then he removed his eyepiece and turned to me. "Right. Now listen carefully Potts, because I'm only going to say this once. You can get off to Vancouver, that's in Canada if you don't know, as soon as you like. Book into a hotel called the Regency, it's close to the airport. You will be contacted there. An arrangement will be made with you to hand over Bexley. That's it, drop dead, and don't bother following me." With which he started to walk past me.

I did a quick side step and got in front of him. "Not so fast Peter."

He gave me a surprised look, but he recovered fast, "So you know my name. Well, I know yours…Pisspotts, so we're even. Move your body."

"Even? You got rocks in your head; you're not even close…I'm way ahead."

"What the hell is that supposed to mean?"

"Means, for starters," I started to pull the recorder out of my pocket, and let him see me switch it off, "I have our conversation on this tape."

He made a grab for it, and I tested the muscles of his solar plexus with a fast jab to his midriff. Which diverted his intentions; he appeared to get a fixation about sucking air. That proves a track-suit does not an athlete make.

I used the time during his breathless period to explain: "You're in the shit Hepworth. I also had some photographs taken of you at the palace just now—you might think of them as mug-shots."

He swung his bag at my head…and blew it, he chose a side swing…much too slow, I ducked with time to spare. As the bag sailed over my head, I reached up and grabbed his wrist as it was going by. Grasping his elbow with my other hand, to stop it turning, I broke his arm over my knee.

He went pale, looking quite ill. He looked unwell enough to be laying down, so I kicked his legs out from under him.

Not surprisingly he dropped the bag. I retrieved it, took out the diamond loaded book, then tossed the bag into the lap he made as he sat up.

I squatted down beside him in a matey manner. "So how d'you like them apples?" I enquired. "Never learn do you? I just knew you weren't paying attention when I took the trouble to talk to you like a Dutch uncle the first time we met. You should have listened, now you're further up the creek, with only one arm to paddle your way out. I told you, but you were obviously not in a receptive mood, that I didn't give tinkers cuss about bringing you to justice, and I still don't. You can piss off right now as far as I'm concerned. But, if I don't collect Sir Bexley, looking hale and hearty, I go to the police with everything I have. And if they don't nail you, I will. I might get to you before they do, which will be your loss; I'll nail you permanently. So, think on those matters for a second or two; then tell me what the set-up is in Canada. I don't want names, just the situation."

He was in considerable distress by this time, but I'd had the same trouble, with a boot up the arse, so he wasn't getting any sympathy from me.

"Oh Christ," he ground out, "give me my money back," he pleaded.

"Sorry, you gave it to me, remember? No refunds you moron. Satisfaction was neither guaranteed, nor implied"

"I can't pay my people in Canada without it," he hissed between clenched teeth.

"How sad," I commiserated. "Well, I expect you intended to pay them from the proceeds of the diamonds. So fib a bit, don't tell them you ain't got them anymore. Practice being a criminal, con them, make like a big-shot, lisp a bit like Bogart...your problem."

"Oh shit," he muttered weekly. "Get me to a hospital, please, for pity's sake."

I gave him a close-up of my sinister smile. I've practised it in front of a mirror for hours, usually when I'm shaving, and I've got it to the point when it is chilling—I mean really icy. It certainly seemed to un-nerve him.

"I'll do as you say," he eventually moaned. "Just book into the hotel, they'll contact you. I'll tell them everything is OK and to hand Bexley over to you. Now...please get me some help."

"O K, I'll call for an ambulance. Tell them you reached for the moon, and it fell on you. With any luck they'll set your arm in a permanent kink. By the way give my regards to Rowland. Cooke, with an 'e' I believe." Then as I turned to leave, "I'll be leaving for Vancouver tomorrow, so expedite what you have to do, or reap the pain."

I walked away, and looking back at him as I made my way back along the footpath, I saw that he hadn't attracted any attention as yet. Nobody appeared to have witnessed the fracas, or if they had, chose to mind their own business. The stupid sod was still sitting there holding his arm. I wondered if it would cross his mind that he wasn't cut out for a life of crime? Not very likely; he'd put it down to bad luck. He would get a full ration of that, I decided if he didn't make the appropriate arrangements with the people in Vancouver.

Chalky was hanging about in the vicinity of the parked bike, when I arrived back on the Mall.

"Everything under control?" he asked.

"Fine Chalky, but the athlete is still in the park. He was showing me how to do a handstand; fell on his face and broke his arm, poor bugger."

"Come off it mate. Try the other leg."

"Hard to believe I know, but there it is. Look, why don't you amble along to Charing Cross? I'll join you there shortly; meet me in the buffet…we'll have a pint, eh?"

"That'll do me then," he said, and left without further comment. Which is not to say that he moved fast; he never does that.

I stopped the first taxi that came along sporting a radio communication antenna by stepping out in front of it. I wanted to get away from the scene in a hurry. It either had to stop, or run me down. The driver chose in my favour, but only it appeared, to give me an ear full. I cut him short by asking him to call an ambulance, as there had been a little accident in the park. I apologised to his fares, while the driver spoke to his dispatcher. Brief details, were then relayed by me, to him, and into the microphone.

I thanked the driver for his trouble as he made to drive away, but not before he got in a few choice words of his own. "You walk out in front of me again you'd better be wearing that bleeding crash helmet."

The ability to have the last word is I think mandatory in applying for a London hackney cab licence.

I was at the bar in the station buffet before Chalky came puffing in. I ordered a pint for him as he came through the door, and we made ourselves comfortable at a table in the corner.

We swigged a few companionable gulps of our beer before Chalky said, "So, you going to tell me about it?"

It was time to tell, so I launched right in with the tale of Hepworth's invasion of my place last night. I told him everything, except about the boot up the backside. He'd have laughed at my humiliation and I wasn't about to give him that satisfaction.

Timing it nicely, I swigged the last of my beer as I reached the end of my story, which sent him off to the bar for his round.

He returned and set the drinks down, and then I filled him in with the details of today's episode.

"Let me get this straight Harry," he said as I finished. "Are you telling me, that Sir What's-his-Name is as good as free; you've still got the diamonds, and there's ten thousand quid in your pocket?"

"About sums it up," I agreed. "Just the way the cookie crumbles," I added modestly. "I got the breaks."

His face folded up, a pleasure to watch. His lips pressed together, as though he were suppressing a belch, then a grin spread itself across his face. His lips parted; his mouth opened and a roar of laughter bellowed out. He laughed so much his eyes watered. After mopping his face with half a sheet he'd yarded out of his pocket, he regained some vestige of control.

"Broke his bloody arm…" he managed, which set him off again, tears streaming down his cheeks.

"You got the breaks? Oh my God!" he stuttered, almost recovering. Which tipped him over the edge again.

Laughter is infectious; I had to grin a bit. Looking around at the other tables I saw that the mirth was being shared. Fortunately Chalky excused himself and made off in the direction of the Gents.

He returned still wiping his eyes and sat down, his face not too stable. He cleared his throat a couple of times, "So, you're off to Canada tomorrow then? Be almost like going home won't it?"

"No, I don't think I can say that, I've never actually been to Vancouver, but I hear it is in one of the most beautiful settings in the world. Wonderful harbour, with a backdrop of mountains, it is on the Pacific you know. You can fly there now in about 9 hours, the route goes over the North Pole which is quite a lot shorter—small world now Chalky."

"Very true Harry. Hasn't always been that way though. I'll tell you something. When I was about your age I had a friend who went off to Canada. I firmly believed when I said cheerio to him, that it was forever. I think he thought so too. People who went off to those places pretty well had to sell up everything just to pay their fare to get there. Then there was the time it took to do the journey.

"Tell you what," I said, and it was definitely on the spur of moment, "Why don't you come with me?"

"Eh?" he gurgled.

"Why not, you've never crossed the Atlantic. You'd enjoy it. Say the word and it's my treat, or shall we say Hepworth's treat."

"No, I couldn't do that Harry!" He was almost flustered, which could be a first for him.

"Of course you could, just nod your head, nothing to it."

"But you're leaving tomorrow, I couldn't be ready"

"Rubbish, you're ready now, even got your camera."

"No, no, out of the question. I'd be more useful to you here. You wanted me to keep an eye on that Miss Watkins, that's what I'll do."

"Things have changed, no longer necessary. You could be more help to me over there."

"Like doing what?"

A tough question, but the old grey matter did its stuff. "Ah, well, I should think that would be obvious." I said, wishing that it was obvious to me. "Let's put it this way. How much help would you be if I got into trouble while I was over there, and you were here?"

"Hmm," and a lot of silence.

"Passport up to date," I asked.

"What? Yeah...I think so."

"That's settled then, all set for the morning; you and me Chalky, off to beard the villains in their lair. Poor buggers think I'm coming alone, they'll never know what hit them when you pop out of the woodwork."

"What time tomorrow? I'd have a lot to do you know."

You've got the rest of the day. How long is it going to take you to pack a toothbrush? I'll pick you up at seven in the morning. How would you like to travel to the airport; in the Bentley or on the back of the bike?" Which in the selling game, is what they call a dual positive suggestion—whichever way the sucker jumps…you win.

"Bring the Bentley," he chose. Which I knew he would, I only ever managed to coax him on to the pillion of the bike once, he didn't speak to me for a week after.

"I'd better not hang about here then," he said and hurriedly finished his pint. "Christ Harry, I'm all of a tizzy. I think I'm in shock, me going to Canada, just like that, I don't know where to start."

"Start by getting the film developed, then by the time you get home you'll have it all sorted out, what to pack I mean. Don't bring your winter woollies, despite popular beliefs there are not too many Eskimos in Vancouver."

"Right, no Eskimos; and get the film done. I'm off then. See you in the Rose tonight?"

I agreed that that was a good possibility, and he left shaking his head.

I phoned Lady Bexley before leaving the station. I didn't confuse her with all the nuts and bolts of the situation, keeping it simple by saying that I had been contacted by the kidnappers and would be leaving for Canada in the morning.

I assured her that she would be the first to know when her husband had been released. To her question of when did I think that would be, I told her that with any luck Sir Aubrey would be a free man; and possibly phoning her himself within 48 hours. She was terribly excited and although I derived much pleasure from her high spirits, I admit to having some qualms in making what could easily be an over optimistic prediction.

CHAPTER EIGHT

Heading for home after leaving Charing Cross, I gave the bike a good work out and arrived back at my cottage in time for a late lunch-come-afternoon tea.

Mrs. H., who was still pottering about when I pulled in, rustled up a meal of cold ham and salad while I showered off the sweat of London.

While I was eating I saw that Taffy the gardener was drifting over the lawns with the mower. So I took my final cup of tea, along with one for him, and walked across to tell him how well the garden was looking. He's a nice little chap, who thrives on praise, a commodity that costs nothing, so he gets a shovel full from me at regular intervals.

Then, with the sun still showing off, as though it had slipped its mind that this was England, I thought I'd give it something to shine on by stretching out on one of the garden lounges. I do enjoy the occasional cigar, and as I thought the day had gone rather well I rewarded myself by lighting up.

Laying back in a haze of cigar smoke I relaxed in a comfortable aura of well-being, contemplating, with a warm glow of satisfaction, the perks or fringe benefits associated with my profession of Finder. Do as I please; in my own time; travel the world; all expenses paid with a little on the side while I'm doing it…hard to beat, I'd say.

Don't even have to do my own gardening I mused, blowing a smoke ring and watching Taffy as he put his cup down; then get back to guiding the mower in ruler straight swathes. My lawn would give Wembley Stadium a run for its money, and not by the sweat of my brow, which in itself brought forth a sigh of contentment from my lips. Then, to top it all, the satisfactory conclusion to a kidnapping case was peering over the horizon. And, if I played my cards right, there would be enough publicity to put me in the big-league, from whence as they say in that kind of novel, fame and fortune would smile on me.

The sound of a vehicle entering the driveway broke my reverie. I saw at a glance that it was Chalky's car.

What now, I wondered, probably coming to con Mrs. H into minding his cat, while he's away.

He'll be lucky I inwardly scoffed. Mrs. H's favourite critters are not cats, especially Chalky's, which is mangy, with a downright mean streak. It treats any handy leg as a scratching post.

He came directly towards me though, so it wasn't his cat that was on his mind.

"You booked my seat on that plane yet?" he asked without preamble.

"Give me a break," I entreated. "I've barely arrived home yet."

"Don't bother then," he said.

"It's no bother, I'll do it right now," I said quickly. "In a hurry now are we?"

"Don't get up," he waved me down. "That's not what I meant. The thing is, I've changed my mind; I am not coming."

"Why not," I asked, "something happen?"

"Nothing's happened. I've just had time to think about it, that's all. Tell me Harry, how long do you expect to be in Canada?"

"Couple of days should do it; that would be my guess."

"Right, that's what I reckoned. So what am I going to see in that time? Nothing is what. Now don't think that I am belittling your gesture Harry; that's not what I'm saying. I know you meant well. In fact it quite took the wind out of my sails when you made it. But driving home, I got to thinking about it, and that's what I've decided. Anyway there's another thing too, it's too much of a rush for me. It will be for you when you get to be my age. Mind you, at the rate you dash about there's not much chance that you'll ever reach my age. So, anyway, that's it, that's what I came to say, and don't try your usual flannel. My mind's made up. And now I wouldn't say no to a cup of tea."

"I'm shattered Chalky," I offered, "I was looking forward to your company."

"That's all I would have been too; company. Nothing over there I could do for you, I'd be like a fish out of water."

I thought he was probably right. Trying to convince him otherwise didn't seem promising, so I took him into the kitchen and drank some more tea with him. Over which he insisted on driving me to the airport in the morning. An offer I accepted with an outward show of appreciation and an inward feeling of trepidation. He drives like he moves, slowly.

Then I was called to the phone, where I took a call from an intimate friend. A lady invited me to dinner…and suggested I bring a toothbrush. This is a lady who knows a thing or two about passion, and excels at lusty farewells.

I'd barely wiped the smirk of anticipation off my chops when I got back to the tea and chatter with Chalky. He went straight away into the snaps he had taken at the Palace, which were, he said, being developed and printed at this very moment. So we'd be able to study them at the Rose this evening, where, because of my departure on the morrow we would have a bit of a bash.

Now I am really quite fond of Chalky. If pressed, I might say that I truly care for the old bugger. But, one has, I felt, the right to draw the line when the demands of friendship threaten to stand in the way of the demands of the flesh.

The thing was; how to convey kindly, that his bid for my companionship this evening had as much chance of being snapped up, as a mismatched pair of dentures at an auction.

I was forced to lie.

"Sorry old mate," I said. "But that phone call I just took was a client, who is most anxious to see me this evening."

"Haven't you got enough on your plate, to be going on with?" he replied; a touch on the huffy side I sensed.

"This is more of a public relations visit, and you know how important that is Chalky; in fostering future benefits." I like to stay as close to the truth as I can—complicated lies are hard to remember. "And," I went on, encouraged by the thought. "This is one client who is going to roll some business in my direction."

He seemed to buy that.

He left, reaffirming his intention of picking me up at seven o'clock in the morning.

"Better make that six-thirty," I suggested.

* * * *

This worked out to be a shrewd guess, because when he came tooting into my driveway the following morning, I'd only just arrived home. So with the bag I'd packed the evening before, I sauntered out to meet him, and what he didn't know thwarted the inevitable lecture on my morals.

We had a conference during the journey. The photos had turned out well; had caught a good likeness of Hepworth. I brought up the matter of the possible bug on the Bexley phone, and what if anything need be done about it. Chalky uncharacteristically volunteered to have a go, no doubt to justify his not coming with me to Canada. Concerned about the adequacy of his expertise as a bug-swatter, I suggested he should get the phone company, to inspect the line and phone on the pretext of a routine maintenance call.

When he dropped me off at the Departures entrance, I declined to invite him for breakfast as he had used up most of the time I'd allowed as a buffer before my flight time. He did make some light-hearted quips warning me about not going around mugging people in Canada, the Royal Canadian Mounties might be offended, and to be careful about biting off more than I could chew.

I said I'd let him know if I did, so he could get a bellyache laughing. The typically British good-bye, where both parties manage to convey the impression that they could care less, and were pleased to see the back of each other anyway.

I gave him a wave as he drove away, I felt I'm allowed to show a small token of emotion-as I'm only half British.

He gave me two fingers, in an upward sweep, for my trouble.

V for victory, or 'up yours', I pondered, but not for long. In a trice I was caught up in the frenzy of petty formalities that precede the boarding of a plane.

Boarding a plane should be as easy and casual as catching a bus, but I've never found it so. Mind you-I thought, as I followed a stewardess up a spiral staircase to an upper deck, planes are getting to look more like buses. All she needed to complete the scene was a ticket machine slung round her neck and be calling out, "Pass right along the bus please."

The atmosphere was all wrong for a bus though; soft lights and hushed voices with pastel tones and plush seats; with the strains of muted celestial music gently caressing the ears.

All contrived, I thought, with a pang of anxiety, to make one feel they're in heaven before we even leave the ground.

If I have conveyed the impression that I'm a white-knuckle flyer, I've got it right. However; making my way to the seat indicated on my boarding pass, I slipped my casual bored-by-it-all mask on and proceeded to stuff my bits and pieces in the overhead locker. I have wondered in idle moments if I could keep that mask on during a screaming nose-dive. Would I still have it fixed in position when we ran out of sky? Certainly a question to ponder on!

I sweated it out as we thundered along the runway in a lumbering giant that was obviously much too heavy to ever leave the ground. Of course it did, I knew it would, I always do when it's done it.

The cabin crew entertained us as we gained altitude, by drawing our attention to the fact that we would be flying over water and demonstrating the correct way to use a lifejacket. Pointing out also, which emergency exits would be our best bet if we needed to vacate the premises in favour of a dingy. As most of the journey was going to be over the pack ice of the Arctic, I found it difficult to drum up a lot of enthusiasm. Paddling a rubber boat about between ice-floes is not something that is likely to grab my interest for too long.

As is the custom of airlines; having exposed the customers to gloom and doom by illustrating what could happen if they foul up, they switch to the party mode and ply the booze.

By the time I had imbibed my second drink, I'd decided that I was in good hands—a thoroughly competent crew, flying a very safe aircraft. The stewardess was a doll, my fellow passengers were jolly good sorts, and flying really was spiffingly good fun.

So I settled back and gave some thought to what problems might await me in Vancouver. I didn't spend much time on that. It was an exercise in futility I decided...until I heard from the kidnappers. With that resolved I went to sleep.

I passed the rest of the flight between naps in a haze of eating, reading, crossword puzzles, and the odd chat with fellow passengers.

In no time at all it seemed, the 'fags out' and 'belt's on' signs were flashing and pinging and we were coming in for a landing.

We touched down with the usual thump, and once again the undercarriage didn't fold, much to my surprise. Then with much rumbling and roaring we trundled about a bit before coming to rest. The mad rush started, as though we were competing for some kind of rebate, for being first off the plane; travelling companions becoming strangers again.

I was well back in the pack getting off. I got stuck behind a rather large elderly lady. As I couldn't get past her, I decided I might as well give her some help. Probably a Mrs. H to someone, so what the hell.

A brisk walk through a seemingly endless tunnel brought me eyeball to eyeball with an immigration official, who asked me if I was planning on staying long. I told him I was on holiday, and would stay until my money ran out, which could be tomorrow. With an imperious flick of his hand he waved me through.

Forward and onward, I went to the roundabout, to try my hand at the "grab-a-bag" game.

Soldiering on to Customs, where I answered that I had nothing to declare. By way of calling me a liar, the officer asked me to open my bag. He had a good rummage. I used the time to get my cigar case out and select a cigar, he looked at the no smoking sign and I rolled my eyes in sympathy.

He didn't take it as a personal affront when he found nothing illegal in my luggage. I didn't show any relief that he hadn't inspected my cigar case. We were even.

Clear of formalities at last, I made a beeline through the crowd towards the exit. As the automatic door opened, finally releasing me from the confines of aircraft and airports, I stopped and took a few deep of marvellously fresh air, the first since leaving London. It felt so good-I lit a cigar.

I stood at the entrance for a minute or two, smoking and eyeballing the local scene. The multi-coloured cabs looked a bit bigger and longer, with more chrome than I remembered.

The brightness of sky and air rang a familiar bell; is there anywhere that has clearer air than Canada? As I looked further a field I saw that clarity of visibility I often think of when I remember Canada. The distant mountains to the north of the airport were displayed in such detail they seemed almost unreal, the peaks and valleys forming a sharp-edged irregular frieze to the horizon.

Very nice it looked too, and so much for that I thought, now back to business. On with the quest to find Bexley...with a quick look for a bit of fame and fortune along the way.

I approached the first cab in the line and reached for the door handle.

"Where to?" questioned the driver.

When I stated my proposed destination, the Regency Hotel, he became quite eloquent. His views were presented simply, and to the point. It seemed that, as my proposed destination was so close, he did not consider me a desirable fare.

I told him he was breaking my heart.

He told me to "Take a walk."

I leaned in his window and tapped some hot ash in his lap.

He made a scene, leaping out then dancing about on the sidewalk and batting at his smouldering flies.

A helpful traffic control chap; one of several bystanders who had gathered to watch proceedings, advised me that there was a courtesy bus which ran to the Regency Hotel.

So I hopped aboard that, and ten minutes later had checked in. The time was 6 p.m.

My room was on the third floor, and faced the river. The Fraser River, or part of it. I had picked a local map up in the foyer, and it looked as though the bit of the river I was overlooking was a tributary called the Middle Arm. Which was about two hundred yards wide where it passed in front of my window, and both banks looked to be totally occupied by boat marinas.

Directly below my window the swimming pool sparkled in the late afternoon sun. Around the pool an assortment of bodies were laid out lapping up the suns rays; a couple of scantily clad female torsos showed some promise-but from three floors up it was hard to check the fine print.

A ramp led down from the pool area to the docks of a marina. It looked as though it could be part of the hotel's facilities. Pleasure boats of all shapes and sizes were tied up in ranks along the wide and well laid out floats. At a rough guess, I'd say there were several hundred boats, ranging from runabouts to yachts.

Resolving to wander down there a little later and take a closer look at the attractions, I phoned the desk and asked them to give me a call in a couple of hours.

Then, as a sop to jet lag, I stretched out on the bed and switched off.

CHAPTER NINE

The ringing of a bell switched me on again, but only half-on. I scrabbled to get a finger-hold on reality. Bell?...alarm or phone? Taking a swipe at where the alarm should be: eliminated that; it wasn't there. Had to be the phone...I was waiting for a call...Bexley...kidnappers...the hazy thoughts floated past. I found the phone, and then mumbled my thanks for the wake-up call.

"Vulnerable Harry, get with it!' I told myself. So taking myself in hand, I gave my body a shower, threw some clothes on it, and aimed it in the direction of the hotel coffee shop.

Two cups of caffeine later, had me raised a notch above sub-human, so I tore out to the pool to see what I could latch onto for the evening.

The bikini set had packed it in for the night. The patio was barren, not a female in sight. I shouldn't have expected anything else. The kind of equipment that had been lurking under those Band-Aids would have been snapped up long before the sun went down. After dark is pop-out time.

Well they weren't going to pop out in my direction, I speculated, that I'd slept my chances away, and finished up empty handed, which did nothing to perk me up.

A couple of kids were splashing about in the pool now, having a whale of a time. I stood and watched them for a while. They ignored me; too busy enjoying themselves. I scowled at the little sods. I would have appreciated some company-any company.

I sulked off, and went down the ramp that led to the marina. Wandering along the docks, admiring some of the moored extravagances lifted my spirits a shade. I enjoy looking at a good boat...that someone else is pouring money into. I chuckled to think what some of them had cost somebody. For a bonus there were the semi-derelicts, waiting for a masochist with a varnish brush. There were even a few work-boats; I mean the ones that earn money. Beside one of these, a chap was standing on the dock coiling lengths of rope into bundles. The name on the stern of the boat was Nocturnal Hooker. I paused wondering how a name like that came about.

I mentally played around with some interesting theories,-some amusing, then got diverted by the ropes the chap was coiling, they had metal spikes spliced into one end.

I looked at the scruffy character who was doing the coiling. Full facial fungus, cut off jeans, no shirt and a chest about a yard wide, and arms which would make a gorilla nervous.

His boat, Nocturnal Hooker, was a matching accessory. It wore the same declaration of brute force. Not that it was a large boat, but it was chunky, almost as broad as it was long. It spotted a wheelhouse up front, which looked like a gun turret, and a brawny looking tow post welded into the centre of the afterdeck.

I stood and watched the bloke; it's always a treat to see someone else at work-when I'm at rest.

He eventually looked up, as people will, when you stare at them. Our eyes met, but all his offered were a pointed stare in return. I was beginning to feel superfluous.

"Evening," I ventured, with nothing to lose. "What are the ropes for?"

"For when I need them," he said; a tad on the ungracious side I thought.

"It's a wise man who knows his needs," I cautioned, in a pleasant enough tone. I'm not cantankerous by nature, but he'd better watch it I decided.

"You from out of town?"

"Yes, as a matter of fact," I replied suspiciously. And then, as he was beginning to look more friendly. "How did you guess?"

"Guess?" Through his beard I caught a glimpse of white teeth, "with an accent like yours?"

Here we go again, I almost sighed…a stranger on both shores. But putting it on a bit for him, I said, "Abso-bally-lutely correct old chap, just stepped off the plane. Names Potts, Harry Potts," and I stuck out my hand.

He took it, and shook it. "Jones, Vic Jones. My old man was from Wales."

"Sang a bit, did he?"

"Yeah, all the time, how did you know?"

"Lucky guess," I said. "I'd still like to know about these ropes."

"Would you? OK…we call them dog-lines, and don't ask me why. They're for towing logs; I'm what you call a beachcomber."

"Really, I thought they walked along beaches, looking for flotsam or something. What's that got to do with logs?"

"Is that right…flotsam eh? None of that around here; this is logging country. Lookit, you see this white flag on my boat," pointing at it. "See, it's got L S written on it. Same on both sides of the boat," drawing my attention to a board attached to the side of the wheelhouse which proclaimed LS 2342. "That means I'm a Log Salver. I hold a permit from the government, to collect free floating logs. Once I stamp my number on a log it's mine. Then I sell 'em back to the logging companies. That's what a beachcomber is."

"Where would these free floating logs come from?" I asked.

"Out of booms, where else?"

"Bear with me old sport," I said. "But what the hell is a boom?"

"You're not kidding me…old buddy?"

"No, straight up, I haven't a clue. But I'd like to find out."

By this time, he had finished coiling his dog-lines. As he tossed the last one into the boat, he said, "If you're really interested, come aboard. We'll get the coffee pot on, and I'll educate you."

And he did, he told me a lot about the life of a beachcomber in British Columbia, plus giving me a good insight into the logging industry.

Here is the gist of what he told me: British Columbia is blessed with millions of acres of trees—fir, hemlock, spruce and cypress. All of which produce lumber (timber) which is readily saleable on the world markets. The province is also blessed with a very long coastline, most of which is protected by a string of islands which form a natural breakwater. Nature obligingly grows plenty of trees along the fringes of these protected waterways. As trees float well on water, a system has evolved over the years of using this floating ability to transport the trees to the mills.

When a tree has been felled and trimmed of its branches, it becomes a log. Logs are roughly uniform; all long and round. Which are easy to make into rafts, and a raft locally, is called a boom.

Fortunately for Vic and his mates, logs don't always stay in booms. Some get water logged and sneak out; some get bounced out by rough seas. Occasionally a boom breaks up, creating a hazard to shipping…there can be several hundred logs in a boom. This is when the beachcombers get a pay-day. Their boats are small and handy enough to get in amongst the scattered logs and retrieve them. The beachcombers provide their own boats; most of them are well equipped. Nocturnal Hooker boasted a ship-to-shore radio telephone. The boats have to be fast, seaworthy, have power enough to spare for towing, and be available twenty-four hours a day if the operators hope to make a living.

I found it all interesting, and during the course of the evening Vic and I got along well together. I admit I encouraged the relationship; he looked like a handy chap to call on, should the occasion arise.

When we parted company, he extended an invitation to come out and see the river sometime. I took his number and told him if time and circumstances permitted, I'd jump at the chance.

Interesting evening, I decided, as I made my way back up the ramp. It is an unusual occupation; being a beachcomber, almost as odd as being a finder. I hadn't run that past him; just told him I was here on business.

My stomach was growling now, I wasn't sure whether it was hungry, or protesting about the coffee intake. Nothing I could do about the coffee, so I found the restaurant and fed my belly. The right decision-it stopped growling.

A couple of drinks later I was back on my bed, preparing to lower myself back into the depths of slumber, and wondering what tomorrow would bring. The hell with it, I was tired. Tomorrow, like any other day, would have to take care of itself.

In a flash it seemed, tomorrow turned into today. My watch told me it was 8:45 in the a.m.

The thought of watches and time, led me to wondering what time, or for that matter what day, I was likely to hear from the kidnappers. Today was a good possibility. I arrived at that conclusion by recalling the time and day I'd twisted Hepworth's arm, figuring out what time he got away from the hospital, subtracting the time zone difference, then guessing what he'd told his accomplices at this end; all logical stuff.

Today then, and with that in mind, I leapt out of bed, and took a cold shower. Boy oh boy, was I going to be ready for them! Not without my morning tea though, my day does not officially start without that.

By the time I'd had a quick shave and dressed, I was really parched. I couldn't spare the time to wait for an elevator, I ran down the stairs. Finding a table in the coffee shop, I ordered emergency tea, the morning paper, and bacon and eggs. As soon as the waitress brought the tea, in a metal teapot with the string of a trapped tea bag hanging out of the lid, I knew I should have remembered. They haven't made a proper cup of tea in North America since the Boston tea party. Mrs. H., I thought, would have tears in her eyes if she could see me now. I almost had tears in mine.

I drank it anyway-well you will, if you're desperate. I scanned the paper as I sipped the sorry stuff, and discovered Canada's problems were more or less the same as England's, a plague of politicians, and other assorted disasters…all of which get star billing. I am convinced there are international schools for newspaper editors, where they get brainwashed into believing-if it's negative, it is news.

The bacon and eggs weren't too bad, but the sports pages were devoid of cricket scores, so I didn't dally over breakfast.

I went to reception and told them I was expecting a phone call, and to page me if necessary.

There were several shops in the foyer, so I had a poke around them. In the gift shop I latched onto a pair of boxer shorts. Not my first choice…on two counts. I am a jockey shorts man myself, I find they give good support-as the bra makers tell the girls. And one doesn't have to worry about which side to dress-as the tailors ask the boys.

But there isn't a lot of spare storage space in jockey shorts, and I needed some. I'd brought the diamonds along with me, just in case. In my cigar case, actually, and I have been known to get careless with that. Wouldn't do to lose the bloody things, hence the boxer shorts. I did say, not my first choice on two counts, well the other count was-they were yellow with black polka dots.

I picked up a boating magazine in the shop next door, and settled down in an armchair in the lounge. I worked through to the classified ads. An ad for a sailboat had my interest, "a sacrifice" the ad claimed. It didn't say who the lamb was meant to be, but I was betting on the buyer. I fantasised that I'd bought it anyway, and was chugging about among some tropical islands in it…when I was paged.

I scuttled to the desk. "Harry Potts'" I told the phone.

"Listen good and keep your mouth shut," it said. "You only get one roll of the dice. What you do is this. Hire yourself a boat from the marina. Tell them you are going fishing, and could be out all night. Later today, go down the North Arm to the mouth of the river. Close to a mile south of the jetty there is a can-buoy. Tie up to it at sundown, and wait. Don't show lights, and make sure you are alone. Wait there for as long as it takes. Sometime during the night, if you do it right, you get the delivery. Foul up, and it all ends right there."

"Now, hold it…" I began, and ended. The click of the phone deprived me of an audience.

I would like to have had a bit of a chat about things, to get the feel of his disposition. But, looking on the bright side, he hadn't mentioned anything about collecting—just delivering. So maybe Hepworth had taken my warning and advice to heart, and whoever his accomplices were at this side of the world, still thought he was going to pay them.

There was one way to find out. Just sit in a boat…perhaps all night, and worry about getting done. I mean, if one knows one is likely to get hammered, fair enough—a chap can plan some nifty footwork. It's when you don't know, that it gets bothersome.

The situation, I reasoned, was after all, of my own making. Now, if I hadn't bent the Morris? But then, as they say, you can't have your cake and eat it too. Although, I have never subscribed to that line of thinking…I think you can!

I'd mulled that over on my way to the marina. Vic's boat was no longer tied up there, so I presumed he was out snagging logs and "making a buck" as he had put it last evening.

The bloke in the marina was a young fellow destined to get on in the world. He did his best, in the nicest possible way, to rent me a forty-footer with enough room to accommodate a harem. It would have needed a Sheikh to afford it. I settled for your basic twenty footer; small cabin; a bit crowded with a sink, stove, and a head. Powered by a Volvo out-drive; it looked like it could go in a hurry.

It also had a decent sized cockpit, which I felt would be an asset, I'd hate to be cooped up in a cabin waiting to see what fate might deliver—I like to see it coming.

The nice young man, once he had accepted that I was not the Sheikh, informed me that there was really everything I needed for a fishing trip, except food. Not everything, I thought, what would be handy, was a concealed cannon. He briefed me thoroughly on the operation of the craft, showed me a chart of the area, and pointed out the best fishing spots. He also gave me a run down on how best to use the fishing gear, which was a cut above a piece of string and a bent pin.

All the best fishing spots he recommended, entailed going down the North Arm of the river, and I made sure that route was indelibly drawn in my head.

I made arrangements with the hotel regarding sandwiches and the makings for tea and instant coffee. I also had them include a bottle of "cheer." My vigil tonight might be lonely, but it wasn't going to be an exercise in discomfort, not if I could help it.

By the time I had finished with the preparations, it was coming up to lunch time.

The only thing left to do was try to buy some insurance.

Vic, my old buddy of last night, seemed a likely broker. First thing to do was contact him, then figure out what to tell him. Any story would do, I reasoned, which would keep him in the vicinity of the can-buoy. Somewhere out of sight but handy enough to come to my rescue if I finished up out of my depth.

Vic's boat was still out, away from the dock, so his phone number wasn't much good to me. Later this evening perhaps, but not now...and later this evening would be too late.

What I needed was a radio. I knew from what he told me last night, that he kept his radio tuned to the commercial channel. Channel 6, I think he had said, I would have paid more attention, had I known that I was going boating.

Then I remembered...he'd mentioned the coffee shop of a hotel across the river, where a table was permanently reserved for the beachcombers. The Horizon Hotel, I recalled, which had me walking across the swing-bridge to the other side of the river. Vic had reminisced about this bridge; apparently at one time it had been the only link between Vancouver and the airport.

Kill two birds with one stone here I thought, as I approached the Horizon hotel. Find another beachcomber, who had a radio in his boat, and also have some lunch.

I found the coffee shop, which led me to the table with the Reserved sign on it. Five chaps were sitting round it, feeding their faces and chatting. My arrival put a stop to both activities.

"I'd like to get hold of Vic Jones," I announced.

They looked me over—I returned the inspection. As shady looking a crew, as you would wish to avoid.

"He's working down river," one of them offered.

"Would one of you give him a call on your radio?" I asked.

"Sure," said the spokesman, "soon as I've finished here," then got his fork back into his French-fries.

"Thanks. Ask him to call Harry Potts. He knows where."

"No problem." Then they were back to their lunches...I had been dismissed.

Moving to an empty table, I ordered lunch. Judging by the size of the specimens at the beachcombers table, the food here would do me.

I finished first, looking across at their table I saw they were still sitting chatting, so as I departed I walked over to their table.

"No rush," I said. "But the call is to Vic's advantage; he'll be grateful." Giving them a nod, I left.

I was in my room, back with the boating magazine, when Vic called.

"What can I do for you Harry?"

"You busy tonight Vic?"

"Depends on what you are offering."

"You're on the water now," I suggested. I could tell it was an "over and out" line, I could hear the click of his mike preceding his comments.

"Right," he agreed.

"Any idea where you will be, say around six this evening?"

"Coming up river; most likely."

"That's great," I said. "I'll be coming down river in a boat I've hired. I'll look out for you, I shall recognise your boat when I see it; I would like to have a chat."

"Sounds good, see you Harry."

"Roger," I said

The thought of all the sleep I looked like missing tonight, had me feeling tired.

I pandered to the feeling and slept for two hours. Then, gathering up the ordered box of sandwiches and assorted beverages, I informed the desk that I would be out fishing most of the night. Never hurts to let someone know where you are...when you don't know what your journey might hold for you.

At five o'clock, after a push-off and a friendly wave from the nice young man, I embarked on my journey into fear.

As the stern of the boat cleared the dock, I eased the throttle lever forward and was quickly chugging along in mid stream. Heading under the temperamental swing bridge brought me to the main channel of the North Arm, where as instructed at my briefing, I turned left. That, for the sticklers on nautical terminology, is port.

As soon as I rounded the corner I began to see evidence of the logging industry. The tide was flooding, and the tugs were busy making use of it to get their tows up river. Each long snake of connected booms of logs were being attended by several small tugs, one with a tow-rope on the front of the snake, and the others giving it a push as needed to keep it all in line.

Now, as I was on the river that Vic had said he would be coming up, I started to keep an eye open for his boat.

I estimated, at the speed I was going I should be at the mouth of the river in about an hour. Add a bit for a chat with Vic, (if I found him) and I should be in the vicinity of the can-buoy a couple of hours before dusk.

I was running into plenty of traffic now, there were quite a lot of booms coming up river, some of which were slowly passing others. Add the odd monstrous scow being moved along pretty fast behind a large tug...things were getting a bit hectic. Several times I was forced to pull into gaps between the booms tied to the rivers banks to avoid being run down. The scows were the worst, they were travelling the fastest, and when they came from behind me they put the wind up me. Some of them were loaded so high with sawdust they appeared to have thatched roofs. It was like watching a thatched factory come barrelling past.

Hopping from one gap-refuge to another slowed my progress down, but gave me the opportunity to have a close look at some of the wildlife on the banks of the river. In one gap, I spent a few minutes watching a heron poised on its long legs waiting for its supper to swim by. It seemed quite indifferent to the hustle and bustle of industry on its doorstep.

In another gap, I got to watch a chap walking about on the logs with some kind of long measuring stick. It was a treat to watch his footwork. The logs were rolling, some even sank when he put his weight on them, but he always kept one step ahead, this seemed to be the secret of his ability to stay out of the water…keep moving!

I progressed down the river in this fashion until I rounded another bend, to see ahead of me a straight stretch of water leading out to the open sea. The end of the river was in sight.

I was beginning to think that I had missed Vic in all the traffic I had been trying to keep out of the way of, when I saw a small boat coming up river towards me. As the distance between us shortened, I could see the boat was flying a white log salvers flag. It looked to be towing something low in the water, which could be logs, and then I could make out the sign LS 2342 on the side of the boat and knew it was the Nocturnal Hooker.

As I swung across river, in a turn which would bring me up astern, I saw that it was indeed logs he had in tow. I adjusted my speed to come alongside; I was getting the feel of my command now, and getting cocky with it.

Vic, who was in the cabin, came out to the aft cockpit to see who the intruder was.

"Got time for a chat?" I called.

"Sure, tie up to me I don't want to miss this tide."

So, in a minute or two, I was sitting in the cabin with Vic, my boat lashed to his, and being taken back the way I had come.

"So," questioned Vic, "what are you doing out here? In a rented boat yet!"

"A long story," I said evasively, "which I won't bore you with. What I would like to know, is can I rent you for the night?"

"Rent me? To do what?"

"You and your boat actually," I said, "to kind of stand by."

"Stand by what?"

'The can-buoy; the one I hope is just out there past the jetty."

"You're gonna have to tell me more than that Harry. I know where the godamned can-buoy is, but stand by it to do what?"

"Ah," I said, rolling my eyes a bit for effect, "I wish I knew. Look Vic, this is all part of the business I'm in Canada to transact. I had a phone call this morning, telling me to meet someone tonight at that buoy. Someone, I'm not sure I can trust; someone who might just want to do me a mischief. What I want you to do, is to be as handy to that buoy as you can get, without being visible to whom ever it is I'm meeting. Then, if I yell, you come running fast."

He took of his baseball cap, then scratched his head a while and looked like he was mulling things over. "Don't sound legal to me," he decided.

"Oh, no, no, nothing like that," I blustered. "All absolutely on the up and up, in fact you might say you'd be on the side of law and order." Then added before I went too far in that direction..."What would you charge me to stay around for the night?" Money talk usually diverts the mind from dwelling on dicey ground.

It worked. "Three hundred bucks," he said looking me in the eye, "that includes muscle if needed...but any shooting, and I'm out of there!"

"Shooting," I almost shouted, "don't even think about it;" sincerely meaning it.

"I won't be near enough to hear you yell," he said, apparently already getting his mind on business. "The nearest I can get, without being obvious, is the river side of the jetty. It'd take me maybe three or four minutes to reach you from there too."

"Make a lot of noise while you're coming," I suggested.

"You got a flashlight?" he asked.

I shook my head, "Never thought of it."

He rummaged in a locker and produced one. "Take this, any sign of trouble, point it towards the jetty and give me a flash." Then, after reflecting, and still poking around in the locker, "Here, blow on this as hard as you can," he said, handing me a whistle. "I might not be looking when you flash the light. What the hell, do both. You know what kind of boat is coming out to meet you?"

97

"No idea."

"Or what time?"

"No…sometime during the night though."

I handed him three hundred dollars-a hundred and fifty quid…give or take. My peace of mind thought it was cheap.

"I'll be on station; soon as it's dark," he confirmed.

As I was rapidly losing ground by being pulled up the river, I hopped into my boat, cast off; made a turn and resumed my journey.

The banks of the river slowly crept further apart as I progressed towards the open sea. The left bank merged with the heaped up broken rock that formed the jetty. I steered towards that side of the river, following the line of rock, and rounded the end of what was obviously the North Arm Jetty.

To the right, the treed bluffs, which my map informed me was Point Grey, passed astern, giving me a spectacular view of English Bay. In the distance, I was offered a view of the glass and concrete skyline of Vancouver, together with its perimeter of impressive mountains, the whole scene brushed in a delicate pink by the setting sun. Ah me; the life of a finder don't get much better! The sea, bless it, was like a millpond.

I scanned around and soon spotted the can buoy; well named…it looked like a can. Tucked out of the way of the river traffic, and sheltered by the jetty, it made a convenient tie-up for the tugs to transfer or park their tows. There was nothing tied up to it right now.

A few pleasure boats were puttering slowly about in the vicinity, fishing rods pointing skywards from their sterns.

I found an open space for myself; fired up the stove, put the kettle on, stuck a rod in a holder, tossed a weighted line over the side, and did my best to look like just another fisherman.

I knew I wasn't going to catch a fish-there was no hook on my line. In the position I was in, I could relate to some poor bloody fish smacking its chops over a juicy looking piece of bait…and getting a hook in the gums for its trouble.

The bait dangling in front of me was Bexley. Get my hands on him…make a triumphant return to England…Potts had it made.

Banner headlines, Harry the hero; I could see it all. Money and perks; pouring in from all over. No, no hook in the gums for me-I was going to watch those bloody kidnappers like a hawk.

Pity Chalky hadn't come with me I thought, as I waited for the kettle to boil. I would have put him in the boat with Vic. Chalky would know when to send the Marines to the rescue; he had a nose for that sort of thing. I wasn't so sure about Vic.

Time passed pleasantly enough as I chugged to and fro, drifted a bit with the tide, swilled lots of coffee, munched on a sandwich, and enjoyed a cigar. I watched the other fishermen catching the odd salmon, then as light began to fail, saw them reel their lines in and head for home.

Half an hour or so after the last one had departed I tied up to the buoy. The last waning light of the day still lingered on, seeming reluctant to let the mantle of night descend.

Soon I could barely make out the vague outline of the jetty. Fortunately the end of it was clearly marked by a flashing beacon, which would help me to keep my bearings when it got totally dark. The distant lights of the airport cast a faint glow in the sky. Out to sea several lighthouses, which I guessed were located on the offshore islands, were sending their warning messages to mariners. Looking at their intermittent flashes, and wondering what they all meant, helped to pass the time.

The hours passed, each longer than the last. The feeling of tranquillity suggested by my surroundings when I first tied up to the buoy had long since evaporated.

The bones in my backside had grown points. The cockpit was too small to do much other than sit. The last cup of coffee had gone cold on the locker beside me. I had even wasted a dash of Scotch in that one, in an effort to stimulate its appeal. It was getting chilly, there was dampness in the air…and I was pissed off. I debated whether I should have a good belt of neat Scotch, and to hell with it, or keep my wits about me by staying sober and getting colder.

Suddenly the decision was unnecessary; company was arriving. It came in the shape of a floatplane…something that had never crossed my mind. It was on me before I knew it, with a snarl of its engine, then a swish as the floats cut through the water as it skimmed past me at the end of its landing approach.

It turned and came towards me, coming up against the tide. As it inched closer I was mesmerised by the viciously whirling propeller. I backed away on the opposite side of the cockpit, one foot on the side deck, ready to abandon ship if that lethal fan came aboard. The propeller slowed, the plane stopped, a delicate balance between tide and thrust.

What now I wondered, but not for long.

"Cast off," a voice shouted from an opening door on my side of the plane.

Moving stealthily on to the bow of my boat, I grabbed the line and pulled the boat up to the buoy. Then did as I was told…I cast off.

The boat naturally drifted off with the tide. The pilot of the plane timed it well by cutting his motor off as I drifted towards the plane.

As the boat and plane, drifting together now, touched hull to float, a figure emerged from the now opened door. He stepped down on the float and held out to me the end of a line. Through a scarf over the lower part of his face, I caught the words, "Make this fast to your boat."

That seemed reasonable, so I grabbed the line with both hands.

Big mistake…I had put myself in a position of no recovery. Shit, I thought…then stopped thinking.

CHAPTER TEN

As my senses endeavoured to stage a comeback, my memory suggested I had one hell of a hangover.

My senses argued that there had never been a hangover this bad. Whatever it was, my senses insisted, had to be terminal. "You're on your way Harry" they said sadly, "Your bag is packed."

Before I could plead my case, my head began to spin, and then the rest of me started to go round with it. I was lying on a giant turntable, which was spinning faster and faster. My stomach wasn't going to put up with this much longer. I struggled to sit up; so I could throw up.

I won my struggle then lost it in a great spewing of vomit, which left me in a cold sweat. I sat waiting for recovery...or death. Either one would be an improvement.

The two of them fought it out in my head and stomach. One moment, recovery seemed to be getting the upper hand, but then death got in a good one.

Recovery prevailed; nausea loosened its grip, and settled for occasional spells.

I tried my eyes out, to see if they worked. I chanced a quick peek, not that I cared where I was. It was more of an experiment; to see if I could open my eyes and not start spinning again. It seemed all right so I blinked a few times.

A face swam into my vision.

"Feeling better?" it enquired.

"Better than what," I asked, wiping by mouth with the back of my hand.

Then it all came back to me, as the chap said when he peed up wind.

The boat, the wait, the plane and the belt on the noggin...so much for Vic, and my hundred and fifty quids worth of insurance.

"Who are you?" I asked the face, which had stopped swimming. With my eyes back in focus, I looked him over. A sixty year old hermit, down on his luck...I answered my own question. A battered suit, which had seen better days before the Sally Anne passed it on; the trousers held up by a blue and white striped necktie, knotted round a well fed waist. A tall heavyset chap, who right now was standing over me, and looking down at me, from a face that badly needed a razor.

"I am Sir Aubrey Bexley," he announced.

"I'll be damned," I said. "Nice to meet you, I'm sure," then added, as an afterthought, "Where the hell are we?"

"I've no idea, where the hell we are," he replied with more than a hint of irritation. "I was hoping to God you would tell me."

I gave my eyes a work-out by aiming them around us, to see if they knew where we were. They registered a gritty beach; which I was sitting on, and a large expanse of water that looked like a lake. A flat shimmering pool surrounded by trees of the evergreen variety. My eyes suggested it was all new to them. "If you want an opinion," I offered, "we're somewhere in Canada, any idea how we got here?"

"Does it matter, how we got here? The thing is...why are we here? And perhaps you'll be good enough to tell me, who you are?"

"Ah," I croaked, "if I can get to that water, we'll talk." Erecting myself into a near-enough standing pose, and checking that my moving parts worked, I staggered off down the beach. Reaching the water, I waded into it. Leaning forward, I made a scoop of my hands and bathed my head. It was cold…but felt so good. My head had a fair sized bump on in, which wasn't keen on being touched and was still bleeding a bit. I washed my mouth out; the water was fresh, so I drank some.

As I turned and came out of the water, Bexley stood scuffing his shoes about in the wet sand. "You were sick over my shoes," he said, explaining.

"Sorry about that," I said, giving him what was probably a sickly grin. "I'm Harry Potts by the way. I came to rescue you."

"Did you indeed, well you'd better get cracking Potts, because you haven't managed it yet."

"Name's Harry, what do I call you?"

He looked at me a bit hard; then curled a lip in what could have been the hint of a smile. "Under the circumstances, I suppose," he made a gesture at the scenery, "anything you bloody well like. But Aubrey will do."

I offered him my hand. "OK Aubrey, glad to have caught up with you."

"You'd better tell me about it," he said as we shook hands.

So we sat down on the beach, and I told him. From when Lady Bexley had contacted me, to my lapse at the can buoy.

He heard me out without comment. As I finished, he accurately summed it up. "What a cock-up," he pronounced.

He could have been kinder, but I guessed he'd had his problems too. I was anxious to hear about them, so I asked him.

This is the gist of what he told me:

Arriving at Vancouver Airport, he had been met by a uniformed driver, who intimated he was from the mining people Sir Bexley was there to meet. The driver had carried his luggage to the car, opened the door for him then as he lowered his head to get in, had given him a shove. Someone in the car grabbed him and clamped a pad of chloroform over his mouth. The next thing he knew, he was waking up in a log cabin. And that was where he had been until last night.

The cabin had been furnished with a cot and a chemical toilet. A supply of food and fresh water had been there from the start, and had been replenished twice through the partially opened door by a chap in a mask. There had been no window in the cabin, the only light coming from a stock of candles. The walls were of whole logs, at least two feet thick, which were tightly fitted together. The roof was flat, and formed by the same sized logs. The door had resisted his best efforts to break, or burn it down. He had almost asphyxiated himself with the arson attempt; had been forced to use some of his precious water supply to quench the blaze. The cabin was obviously located in a remote area, as the only sounds to penetrate his prison, were those of the wild. Except, preceding the delivery of supplies, when he had identified the sound of a plane. Included in the last delivery which arrived late yesterday was a bottle of Scotch. He'd got stuck into that, but one shot had flattened him; obviously spiked.

He had regained his senses, stretched out beside me, as dawn was breaking, about an hour before I decorated his shoes.

So there we were; the two of us, sitting on a beach facing a lake, knowing not where. The lake was not a puddle…it was at least a mile wide, and a lot longer in length. From where we sat, on the mile wide shore, the end of the lake was obscured by the morning mist, which made it difficult to estimate its true length.

We were talked out it seemed, and I imagined, both occupied by our own thoughts. Mine were pretty basic, mainly concerning my lack of well being. I reached the conclusion after recalling several mornings that I'd felt a lot worse, that I was feeling better. On those occasions though, my misery was self-inflicted, so I didn't make a big issue of it. My body didn't know who inflicted the misery, so it could be just another morning I decided.

These illuminating thoughts were interrupted…

"So how do you assess this situation Harry; why leave us in this place?"

"Good question," I admitted, more in the way of waffle, while I gave it some thought. "This bloke's a client," was one of the thoughts, wouldn't hurt to look like I knew about this sort of stuff. So I reasoned it out…out loud.

"This is the way I see it," I said. "There are many logical reasons, of course, for us being air-lifted to this scenic setting."

"Air-lifted, what makes you thing we came by air?"

"See those tracks on the beach." I pointed them out.

"I see them, so?"

"I'd say they were made by our heels, as we were dragged up the beach. The footprints, no doubt were made by the bastards who dragged us. Notice also, the tracks run from the water to where we were laying. Now you said you recovered consciousness at dawn. I got hit on the head, no more than two hours before that. At which time the kidnappers were in a plane, and I'd bet money you were in the plane too, but drugged. After they thumped me and dragged me aboard, they must have left in a hurry." I was about to mention Vic waiting in the wings and coming roaring out, as a reason they left in a hurry, but realised I never had the chance to alert him

"So," I went on, "I'd say we are somewhere within two hours flying time of Vancouver, which is quite a walk. To get back to those logical reasons why…I can think of two, right off the top of my head. One of which is good; the other is bad. The good one is, we have been released and will find some sort of habitation close, from where we can get back to Vancouver. You want to hear the bad one?"

"Might as well. The last one is not very likely. They could have tossed me into your boat; would have achieved the same thing, and saved them the bother of flying us here."

"True, up to a point," I conceded; glad to note that he was paying attention. "But, on the other hand, by bringing us here, they get a lot more time to make themselves scarce; should we report the matter to the police."

"I'll grant you that," he sounded sceptical. "Let's hear the bad one."

"We were abandoned a long way from civilisation, in the belief we would hike round in circles-until we were dead."

"I like your first theory best, let's work off that."

"Let's stay with the last one. Tell me this; anything left in your pockets that would identify you?"

"Not a damned thing, they cleaned me right out, as you can see," sticking his thumbs behind the tie round his waist, "even pinched my belt...wait a minute, I think I see what you mean. It had a monogram on the buckle."

"That figures," I said, "both our watches too."

"Stripped of all identity, as they say," he said morosely. "Not going to find anyone living here, are we?"

"Unlikely," I agreed.

"So what do we do?"

"Get off our butts. Look, I really hate to mention it, but you were locked up with a chemical toilet a long time. You whiff a bit. So why don't we go for a swim, freshen us both up. You go that way, I'll go the other. When we've cleaned up, we'll decide what to do, all right?"

"Sorry about that old chap," he muttered, looking down at himself, "I had no idea. Must be true, what they say about the fox being the last one to smell his own hole."

Walking off along the beach I formed the opinion that old Aubrey was a pretty decent sort. Not too many blokes, when you tell them they stink, take it that well. Could have got stuck with a lot worse, I thought.

Stripping off, leaving my clothes in a pile, I took a run into the water and plunged in. I'm not going to use the expression "took a header" my head was too tender to contemplate the thought. The water was numbing...what had seemed refreshing when I bathed my head earlier, was now teeth-chattering. I churned along with a crawl-stroke, but not for long, just enough to sluice me off. I ran back out, faster than I'd run in!

Emerging from the water shivering, I jogged along the beach to get the circulation going. The sun was high enough now, I felt the warmth of it, and running about in the starkers quickly had me warm and dry.

Feeling invigorated, and certainly fresher, I looked along the beach to see how Aubrey was getting on. He was doing much the same as me, so I trotted along the beach to meet him. We met about halfway between our two piles of clothing.

We looked each other over, as two males in the buff will. A question of comparison, I suspect. Although, neither one of us had much to use as a yard stick…cold water does that! The rest of him looked to be in pretty good shape though, for an older gentleman that is. I saw, under the unshaven grey whiskers that he wore the clipped military style of moustache. His cheeks had a ruddy glow, which put together with the moustache; the erect bearing of his straight back and shoulders; stamped him unmistakably—soldier.

Our eyes met during the inspection, and we grinned at each other.

"Feeling better?" I smiled.

"Better than what?" he chuckled.

We chuckled together. The ice was broken.

"All we need now," I suggested, "is a bloody good breakfast; we'd think we were on holiday."

"Be nice," he agreed. "Which brings us, I suppose, back to our problems."

"One of them is starvation, if we don't start heading out of here."

"Which way though, that's the question."

"Pick any direction, as long as it's along the lake shore. Anyone living in a remote area is likely to be close to the lake. And anyway, if we walk along the shore, we can't get lost."

"Makes sense, come on, let's get dressed and have at it." He walked back to his clothes, and picked up his underpants between a finger and thumb. "God," he called to me, "I hate to put these bloody rags on again. I could smell 'em myself the last time I passed them."

"We'll do our laundry in the lake," I shouted back, "when we stop for the first coffee break."

I walked back to where my clothes were laying, got dressed and returned to where Aubrey was gingerly stepping into his trousers.

"I've got something to show you," I said, dropping my pants as I talked.

His eyebrows twitched a bit, but he kept his voice unruffled. "I rather thought you just did."

"You'll find this more interesting," I promised, fumbling the bag out of the outrageous polka dotted shorts.

"Wouldn't be my first choice…"

"I'm not modelling the sodding shorts," I interrupted. Holding out the chamois leather bag, I shook it in front of his face.

"Good God, I think I know what you have there."

"You should, I understand you're in the business."

He took the bag and opened it, shaking some of the diamonds out on his hand. "I hardly believe this; how on earth did you manage it?"

"Nothing to it," I said modestly. "All it takes is a brilliant mind, trained in the art of duplicity. The kidnappers are amateurs, they took everything I had in my pockets, but never looked any further. They should also have taken the time, when they phoned, to negotiate. Professionals would. Silly sods fired the message at me, then hung-up fast. I never got a word in. If they had talked to me, who knows, they might have got it all."

"Negotiate?" he questioned, "Might have got it all? What the deuce are you prattling on about Harry?"

That's often a problem with me…running off at the mouth. But considering the plight we were in, there didn't seem much point in not telling him about my meeting in St. James' Park with Hepworth, and the ten thousand quid involved therein.

So I told him.

"Don't you think you put me in rather a dangerous position?" He was miffed…I could tell. His lips were stiff as he spoke, his little clipped moustache did its best to bristle, and his ruddy complexion got ruddier.

"Well we're here aren't we?" I hastily added "almost free."

His face went so red; I started to worry. I know older people are prone to heart attacks in situations like this, and I certainly didn't want to lose him at this stage. I watched him closely; he seemed to be weathering it.

"Precisely," his pointed gaze at our surroundings gave the single word, considerable weight. "Moreover," he accused. "You took a bribe." He gave me the same kind of look I imagined he'd give to a guest who broke wind in his drawing room.

"Bribe!" I retorted…slightly pissed off, to say the least, "nothing of the sort, a business deal, in every sense of the word. We are all in business to make money, right? Not a hobby with you is it? No, I'm sure it isn't, anymore than it is with me. Hepworth invested his money...unwisely, as it turned out. So he blew it. Anyway, think about this. Do you imagine he would have arranged to meet me like he did, unless I had him convinced he'd bought me? Not on your Nellie he wouldn't. All that aside, he made the deal from a strong position—he had me looking up the barrel of a pistol."

He bounced that around in his noggin for a while, without comment. The cardiac arrest seemed to have lost ground. Then he said. "You broke his arm, you say?" He smiled slightly, at least his face relaxed. "Well that's all right then. You provided a service for a fee. There is one point, on which perhaps you'd care to enlighten me. What, in the way of payment, did you bring with you to the rendezvous last night?"

I knew he was going to get upset again, but it had to be told. "The thing is," I related: "After I'd left Hepworth in the park, I couldn't be sure what he had told his people at this end. If he had followed my advice, and told them he was in receipt of the ransom and he'd be paying them shortly, they'd have simply handed you over. But Hepworth looked to be a vindictive bugger, the type that doesn't lose gracefully, the kind of silly sod who might be stupid enough to cut his own throat. So I had to come prepared for almost anything. Apart from your diamonds cunningly concealed among the polka dots, in one jacket pocket I had a bag of agates I picked up in a rock shop, and in the other pocket a bundle of "funny money" I purchased from a joke-shop. It looked a bit like sterling. I thought that as I was dealing with Canadians, they probably wouldn't know the difference—until it was too late. Mind you, I hadn't planned on being unconscious during the transaction, slight miscalculation there. But before you get stressed out again, I suggest to you, that by and large it worked quite well. My pockets were emptied, obviously the faked stuff worked, and you've got the real diamonds in your hand."

And I've still got the real money where it will do most good, I reasoned, but thought it prudent not to bring the matter to his attention.

While I awaited the expected blast from him, I had a sudden thought; a disconcerting thought. I tried in on him for size.

"You realise, in the light of what I have just told you, that our situation has changed somewhat?"

It took him a minute or two to work it out, but I could see by the look on his face that he was getting there. To be honest, it had only just come to me.

"Hell's teeth, yes of course. They will be coming back?" He was already looking furtively about us as he said it.

"Just a matter of time," I should have added, and in a revengeful mood no doubt. I settled for…"Be as well if they don't find us."

We scurried, as one, into the shelter of the dense trees.

CHAPTER ELEVEN

Aubrey took off through the underbrush, like an express train. He'd obviously taken my advice to heart. I stayed close to him at the start, until I took a smack in the chops from a branch whipping back in his wake.

As he was disappearing into the gloom of the evergreens, and I couldn't see out of one eye for tears, I bellowed, "Whoa, slow it down."

He reined in, allowing me to catch up. "I thought we agreed it wasn't a bright idea to run around in circles," I panted. "We lose sight of that lake; the first circle starts. So let us dally a while, and ponder a bit."

"I've no intention of being incarcerated in that filthy cabin again," he puffed, brushing the sweat from his brow with the palm of his hand, while spluttering, "those buggers want to catch me, they better be bloody fleet of foot, and they'll have to find me first."

"My sentiments exactly," I seconded, "and cover we've got. So why don't we go back along this highway you've flattened, and get within sight of the lake. That's if I ever regain my sight, you just about took my flaming eye out with one of those branches. Talking of which, how's your bush-craft? I know you're not strong on stealth," kicking a shattered sapling, in case he wasn't following my drift. "Could you, find your way in a given direction, like west for example?"

"'Afraid not, I could get lost in Kew Gardens. What about you?"

"I've been lost in Kew Gardens."

"I seem to remember," he said thoughtfully, "That moss always grows on one side of a tree; north, I think it is. But I'm not sure. I had plenty of time to ponder on my failings in that department while I was locked up in that bloody shed. I had a pretty fair idea, I was in the wilds somewhere, but I knew if I did manage to break out of the cabin, I had no way of determining a direction to take."

"Which settles that then," I offered. "We don't know our arses from our elbows, so we forget about a trek through the woods. If they don't come back, we'd do better at taking a stab at living off the land. Wonder if there are any fish in the lake?"

"I should think so; it's probably teeming with them. Lot of good it'll do us though. If there are; we've nothing to catch them with."

"Maybe we'd better hope those buggers do come back. Perhaps we can charm them into giving us a ride out," I offered jokingly.

"And how do you propose we do that?" he asked.

"No idea. Try thinking of something," I suggested. "You don't just happen to fly a plane do you?"

"Another of my shortcomings," he answered dolefully. "Can you?"

I rolled my eyes for his benefit. "No, I was in the RAF, but the only thing I flew was a motor bike. Not too accomplished, are we. We could do with a smile from fate."

By which time we had backtracked, so that we could see the lake again. Neither of us it appeared; too keen on leaving the cover of the trees. So as though by mutual consent, we sat down in a partial clearing and lapsed into silence.

I wondered what he was thinking, but quickly lost interest in that.

I knew what I was thinking about...food. Visions of a damned great fry-up, with lashings of tea, kept floating past; teasing hell out of my stomach.

Becoming aware that Aubrey was speaking; the word "commando" dragged my attention from the appetising flick-show my brain was producing.

"...one of my better accomplishments actually," he was saying.

"I'm sorry," I broke in, "my mind was wandering. I missed what you're good at."

"Not bragging, you understand," he said, "merely remarking that I used to be quite handy in the art of killing. Past tense of course, goes without saying, and not the kind of activity one is encouraged to keep ones hand in at, in peacetime that is. I don't think a chap ever forgets though. Now I'm not suggesting we should take such drastic measures in the present situation, not for a minute. But, the thought of applying, shall we say, necessary force, doesn't give me any qualms. No, if the scum do come back, and we can create a favourable situation; you can count me in."

Count him in? I couldn't recall extending an invitation. Just what I needed...like starvation. An old and rusty assassin, trying to get me involved in a remake of the bloody war. "Humour the clot," my instincts told me.

My voice carried on anyway..."Need a few tools of the trade wouldn't you? Piano wire, a fold up bow, and a packet of darts. A stiletto in your sock, and other assorted knickknacks of general mayhem?"

"Improvise...we'd have to use our initiative."

He wasn't displaying any sign of a dampening of the spirit; the silly bugger was serious!

"You mentioned a favourable situation. What kind would that be? Assuming, we get to choose?"

"Create, was a word I also mentioned," he went on. "We create from the circumstances presented to us, which means, we manipulate them to provide the circumstance. To put it simply...you Harry, will distract. I shall, disable."

"Well, that sounds simple enough," I said, which had to qualify for the understatement of the year. I was beginning to have second thoughts about Aubrey.

"In the meantime," I suggested, drawing his attention to the tracks in the sand made by our gallop into the trees, "would it be in order, if we moved to somewhere a bit less obvious?"

"You're getting the idea Harry, one of the basics that; covering one's tracks."

"Only nature can cover those tracks, and that'll take her quite some time. Why don't we go out the way we came in; then relocate, this time without leaving tracks."

"Right, but we leave these tracks the way they are. Lead 'em up a false path, that's the ticket, the hunters become the hunted. You're getting the hang of things Harry."

I was glad to know that.

Aubrey stood up, cocked a thumb in the direction of the lake, and led his one-man army to the beach, this time with stealth.

He stood facing the lake and cast a furtive look in both directions along the shoreline. "Right Harry, off with your shoes, roll up your trousers, and follow me."

With our feet bared, I followed him along the grass, between trees and beach, until we arrived at the trail of footprints I had made going in for my dip. Then fitting his feet in the prints, and following them into the water, he motioned me to do the same.

In the water, we waded in the shallows along the foreshore. Aubrey halted us after a short distance, looking pointedly at a clump of trees that protruded from the shore. "Perfect," he said.

"Looks about right," I agreed in my innocence.

"After you this time," waving his arm for me to lead the way up the beach. He took off his jacket, and as he followed me, swished it behind him obliterating our tracks.

He seemed to be enjoying himself, and 'what the hell' I thought, never hurts to keep the customers happy. Anyway, we didn't have much else to do, in the way of entertainment.

He poked around in the clump of trees, and after rejecting several possibilities, he selected a spot in the underbrush that gave us good cover with a panoramic view of both lake and beach.

"Excellent hide this," Aubrey remarked, from where he'd wandered off to water a tree. "Done much shooting Harry?"

"Not much…unless shooting the breeze counts."

"Wouldn't mind having the pick of a couple of rifles from my gunroom right now," he said somewhat ruefully.

As my armoury consisted of a Diana airgun, with a weak spring, I wasn't inclined to get into a "mine's bigger than yours" session on that subject.

I nodded politely, and changed the subject. "What time do you suppose it is?"

"Shouldn't think it's more than," he was squinting upwards at the sun, "say ten o'clock. Why?"

"Nearly time they came back, if they're coming."

That shut him up; gave him something to occupy his mind. We had a pleasant period of silence, apart from the buzzing of the mosquitoes. It was getting quite hot now, and the little pests were out in force, we must have looked like breakfast to them.

I'd just swatted one that had been buzzing my ear…it sounded like he'd brought his own chainsaw. Then a louder, different buzz, which didn't diminish when I wafted a hand at it, caught my attention.

I looked over at Aubrey; he'd heard it too. He rolled onto his stomach and parted the foliage to get a better view. I followed suit, making my own peephole.

Company was approaching. At first, it was hardly more than a speck which swelled into the clumsy bottom-heavy profile of a floatplane. A menace that swept low over our hide, then roared away over the water. It gained height, banked in a turn then came towards us on a landing approach.

"Must be them eh?" Aubrey said softly. "Better wait and see what they do."

Not much bloody choice, I thought. "Your show," was what I said. "You call the shots."

He nodded, not taking his eyes off the plane.

We watched, as the plane touched down in a cloud of spray, then taxied in a straight line to the part of the beach we had been dumped on early this morning.

The floats grounded on the beach, the sound of the motor died. The door swung open, and a figure wearing a red chequered shirt clambered down onto one of the floats. He was carrying a rifle.

He waded ashore, the rifle held at hip height while he scanned the beach, then stood looking into the trees in front of him. I mentally patted Aubrey on the back for his foresight in moving us.

Another figure emerged through the door, came ashore and joined his companion on the beach. This one had less colour in his clothing, but wore a blue baseball cap. He was also armed with a rifle.

Red Shirt kept his rifle pointed at the trees, while Blue Cap secured the plane by dropping some kind of grapple on the sand.

Then, with both pointing rifles towards where Aubrey and I had previously run into the trees, Red Shirt called out. "OK, you assholes come on out of there."

His voice shattered the silence, we were close enough to receive the message…it came through loud and clear.

"That's the driver. The sod who met me at the airport," whispered Aubrey.

"Get smart. Walk out, or I'm coming in after you," shouted Red Shirt.

When that failed to tempt us, he turned and said something to his companion. Whatever it was, we weren't able to hear. A plan of action I guessed, as Red Shirt commenced moving in the direction of the break in the underbrush. Blue cap stayed where he was, facing the trees with his back to the plane.

"Playing into our hands Harry," Aubrey said softly but urgently. "Made to order; let's do it now. You cut across; get ahead of him. Make sure he gets far enough into the trees, out of sight of the other one. Then let him know where you are. Just get his attention, and make bloody sure you hold it. Leave the rest to me."

"Ta very much," I hissed. "Whatever the rest is, bloody well get it right. I'm too young to die."

"You're wasting time," he hissed back. "Hop to it; no time to lose."

I hopped…in what I hoped was the right direction, trying to work out the angle of interception that would get me ahead of the shit in the red shirt. I moved as quietly and quickly as I knew how.

To keep my mind on the business in hand, I kept a count of my paces. Averaging the short with the long; at a hundred and thirty, I reluctantly decided that if paces were yards, I'd arrived at my appointed position. Adding a few more, for good luck, and my future, I stood up.

Nothing! I looked all around me, still nothing. Where was he? "OK, all right," I commenced to wail. "We give up." The fear in my voice was entirely authentic.

It worked. "Show yourself." My eyes swivelled to where his voice came from; there was still no sign of him. The sound of his voice told me he was close, and the direction it came from suggested he was where I wanted him…between me and the lake.

"We are showing ourselves," I complained in sorrowful tone, while moving carefully towards him. "The old man's in a bad way, I daren't move him."

"Yeah, well move out here where I can see you. Start walking this way. I'm armed, so don't try anything fancy."

I worked my way towards him, making all the noise I could now, shaking bushes and snapping everything in range of my feet. If Aubrey was going to manage to creep up behind our quarry, he'd need all the noise I could raise.

I caught a flash of red ahead of me. "Here I come," I called out, cranking up the volume. "I think I see you now, I'm coming towards you. I've got my hands up. No shooting, please. I'm surrendering. Just don't leave us here." I saw him now; he saw me. I added appropriate facial sorrow to my yelling. "I'll give you anything you ask, please help us," I implored as we approached each other. "The old man needs help desperately, I think he's dying, he looks real queer…"

"Shut your lousy face," he out-shouted me. "Get you act together for Christ sake. All I want from you, you smart assed bastard, is my money. Real money, not that crap you shafted us with."

"Money…I don't understand," I pleaded. "Didn't Hepworth tell you we made a deal?"

"He told me you screwed him; is what he told me, which I don't give a shit about. All I'm interested in is the twenty thousand bucks I've got coming."

"Just take us out of here, I promise you'll get your money," I cut in fast. I had to keep talking. Aubrey was coming up behind him.

"Look," I pressed on, moving closer to him and lowering one hand towards my pocket. "I can…"

"Get your hand back up," he snapped.

"Right," I shot it back up quickly. I had his full attention. At the moment of contact, I winced.

Aubrey had hit him on top of the head, with a length of wood that could easily qualify as a log. He'd delivered the blow two handed in a high swinging arc. I thought the poor sod's head had exploded. I leapt within grabbing range of the rifle, saw his eyes getting glassy then thumped him on the jaw, more from relief than from necessity.

"Is he still with us?" asked Aubrey, bending over Red Shirt's prostrate body and lifting one of his eyelids. I saw, that what I had thought was blood and gore splattering from the head, was in fact, bits of rotten wood. Looking at Aubrey's makeshift club, I saw the reason. The outside of it was rotting away. The core was apparently solid; there wasn't even a twitch from the victim.

"He'll live," diagnosed Aubrey. "Bloody good show Harry, an inspired performance. Come on, no need to waste time on him, he's out of it. Let's sort the other one out before he catches on." He dropped his club and reached towards me. "As you're not much on shooting, will you allow me?" I handed him the rifle.

Quickly checking it over, he jerked his head in the direction of the lake, and set off. I followed. As we glimpsed the reflection of the water through the trees, he motioned me to stay where I was.

Working his way from cover to cover towards the lake, he apparently found the locations which suited him. Raising the rifle, he sighted; then fired. Two down I thought, as the crash of the shot echoed away.

Faulty thinking; you can't talk to the dead. "Stand quite still, and lay down your weapon," Aubrey commanded.

A pause, then he beckoned me and called, "Go and retrieve it Harry." As I passed him, he added, "Stay out of my line of fire."

Keeping to one side, I walked through the trees and stepped out onto the beach. I found Blue Cap standing, near enough where I'd last seen him, this time with his hands in the air. Circling behind him, I reached round and picked up the rifle.

Aubrey strode purposely out of cover and walked up to Blue Cap. I moved forward and joined him.

We stood facing our prisoner. A long lean man saddled with shifty eyes, a narrow face, and a weak chin, a crafty looking bugger, whose eyes darted from one to the other of us, and then to the trees.

"Don't bother looking," I said, taking the initiative. "He's had a nasty accident, he won't be coming out."

"You've done anything to Hank, you'll pay for it." He dropped his hands as he said it.

I backhanded him across the mouth. "No threats." I said, at my most sinister. "They make me, as do lies…irritable. Keep that in mind, and we'll be pals in no time…"

"Tell me about Hank," he shouted. He looked troubled.

"What's Hank to you?"

"He's my brother!"

"He's alive," I would have liked to be just a bit sympathetic; but it never pays. "At least he was a minute ago, but he isn't able to talk just now. So you've been elected. First question: you tell me about Peter Hepworth?"

Dabbing at the dribble of blood oozing from his mouth, he mumbled, "I'll tell you this about him, I wish we'd never heard of the dude. He spun Hank a yarn about this English big shot. Said he was willing to pay big money, to make it look like he'd been snatched. Twenty thousand bucks, he said. All we had to do was stage it like it was the real thing; no chance of any trouble for us. I told Hank it was a crazy deal, but would he listen; no way. At first, Hepworth told Hank we'd get paid after we'd done our thing. Then a couple of days ago he phones, and tells us we get our money from you when you come to collect this guy." He waved a hand at Aubrey.

"Why the muscle at the jetty then, and why abandon us in this place?"

"He said you'd shafted him, said you'd screwed the deal up. Told us it would be better for us, if we got rid of you both. Hank and me are not killers; we dropped you here to give you a chance. Then we find the money's no good, and we come back."

"Nasty man Hepworth," I said, "quite the con artist. You should avoid people like him...no future in it."

"There's no future in it for any of us, if Hank can't fly us out of here," he retorted gloomily.

"You telling me he's the pilot?"

"You got it. That's Hank's thing, I don't fly."

I hoped my face didn't register the despondency within. "You'd better get in there then," I said, pointing the rifle at the woods, "and see what you can do to aid your brother's recovery."

Before misery in a blue cap was lost to sight in the trees, I had the glimmer of a constructive thought. "A radio, you must have a radio in the plane."

"No we don't, must have a radio; it's being repaired," he spat in disgust. "It just ain't been our day."

CHAPTER TWELVE

Aubrey shrugged his shoulders. "I didn't mean to bash him. Intended to go for the pressure points, but you were so damned close, I couldn't take a chance of him getting a shot away."

"Then I'll be eternally grateful that you chose the direct approach." I said, looking at him earnestly. "For my money; you did well. I'll be honest; I didn't think you had it in you."

"Really, well, I have even more reason to commend your courage then. I think that gave me the incentive not to fail."

A glance of mutual respect passed between us. I know I felt it for him at this time. I mean, you do have to admire the old bugger.

It seems to be in the nature of men, that when a feeling of affection surfaces so does embarrassment.

"Hrrm...well," Aubrey cleared his throat, "we're out of the trees. We have the rifles and the plane, but we're not out of the woods yet, are we?"

"Let's go and park ourselves in the plane. We can discuss where we go or don't go from here, just as easily sitting down. Who knows," I suggested, "we could get lucky, there might be some food there."

"Point taken," said Aubrey.

Wading out to the plane, followed by him, I climbed up onto the float and scrambled through the door. It was even a smaller plane inside, than the outside suggested, and that was small. Two seats forward, a pilot and one other. Two smaller seats aft with a bit of stowage space behind them.

Reaching back, I helped Aubrey by taking his rifle, and then gave him a heave up through the door. "Do you suppose the chap was having us on," he said as he inspected the premises, "when he said the other one was the pilot?"

"No, I don't think so, he was pretty rattled."

"Rightly so, I was rattled myself when you hit him. Poor chap must have thought we were a couple of thugs." He was prattling on, while I was foraging for anything edible.

"We are...hey, will you look here!" I gleefully held up a flight bag, with the top of a thermos jug poking through the zip. I pulled out the jug, held it up like a trophy, and passed it to him. Then groping back into the bag I pulled out two packages of sandwiches.

"Manna from heaven," Aubrey chortled.

"After you sir," I nodded towards the front seats. "Lunch is now being served."

Peanut butter sandwiches, not my first choice of filling, but my stomach was long past the point of being picky. We sat in the front seats, eating the sandwiches, and swilling coffee in turns from the thermos.

By mutual consent, it seemed discussion on our predicament was deferred until the very last crumb had been consumed. When, with a discreet burp, Aubrey offered, as he sat back in the seat with a sigh of contentment. "Well, what do you think Harry?"

"I think he told us," I suggested cautiously, "what he believed to be the truth."

"That's as may be. An unlikely tale though, don't you think? I mean to say, all that nonsense about someone offering money to be kidnapped?"

"An English big-shot," were the words he used, I reminded him. "Just about fits you Aubrey, a bit uncouth the description. Nevertheless, not been up to any hanky-panky have you?"

"Of course not, what utter tripe," he retorted.

He sounded convincing. But it wouldn't be the first time I've been wrong about that.

I could see that I'd played hell with his after lunch mood. He'd certainly gone quiet, and I wasn't hearing any more sighs of contentment. But how do you know if a red face indicates guilt, or indignation?

Not that it mattered to me. Messenger right! If I got him home in one piece, I could call it a day. With which thought, the problem of getting home, my own feeling of contentment lost some ground. I wasn't ready for that problem yet, so I let my thoughts idle back, to where I could call it a day. Yes. Now if I could get him back home safely, bearing in mind also that I had salvaged the diamonds for him, I could hit him with a bill for a double finders-fee, him and the diamonds.

With that in mind, I offered a dab of balm to ease whatever emotion had brought the blood to his cheeks. "Sounds like just the sort of false information Hepworth might have tried on them. Probably told them; kidnapping by consent wasn't a crime at all. Maybe it isn't," I mused. "He'd tell a good tale, you can bet your boots on that. Anyway, it's a bit academic. I suppose we ought to see what we can do for the pilot with the bump on his noggin."

Aubrey gave a tut-tut commiseration, at least I presumed it was in sympathy for the pilot. "Feel bad about it now. Given the same circumstances though, I expect I'd do the same again."

"The same what," I like to get things clear.

"The same wallop on the head. I did hit him rather hard, poor chap."

"Stop blaming yourself. You did what was necessary. End of story. So don't worry about it."

"Perhaps you're right." He sounded unconvinced.

"Look," I said. "You stay here and hold the fort I'll go and take a look at him." Getting to my feet, I headed for the door.

"Hold on." He said sharply, offering me one of the rifles. "Don't go in there without this."

"Hang onto them, better for them both to be with you. You've got a good view of the beach from here, so keep an eye on it. Stay in the plane, it's our ace in the pack. We hold the plane; we deal the cards. So just make sure we don't lose the deal."

Jumping down from the float, knee deep in water again, I made a beeline for the opening in the trees. Following, the now well defined trail, I made my way to the (beaning' ground). As I came out into the clearing, Hank was still in the prone position, while his brother sat beside him.

"How's he doing?" I asked, more from hope, than politeness.

He shrugged his shoulders. "What would you think? His pulse is OK, but you've hurt him bad. He hasn't moved."

I bent down and examined the injury. The hair was matted with drying blood, with fresh blood still oozing from a gash. The gash wasn't deep, or didn't appear to be, it was on top of the bump. I've seen worse. I imagined the wood, being soft on the outside, would have softened the blow. It had possessed a solid core though. You can be wearing a foam mat on your head, but if someone whacks you on the head with a sledge hammer...good-night. His breathing seemed a bit shallow, which didn't strike me as a good sign.

"What's your name?" I asked the sitter.

"Don."

"Look Don, I'm sorry about this. It needn't have happened, if you hadn't come at us waving guns."

"Still no reason to hit Hank like this, he wouldn't have shot anyone."

"He should have said. Someone points a gun at you; you expect the worst. We should get your brother to a hospital. You want to take a stab at flying the plane?"

"No, no way. Don't you think I've thought about that? I'd go for it, if I thought it would help Hank. He's safer here. Sure, I've had the controls for a minute or two, but only when we've been well up, and flying straight and level. I'd never get it off the water. Hank's the flyer, always has been. That's all he's ever done. Me, I'm a land surveyor. All I can do is point the way in the right direction."

"How far away from help are we?" I asked.

"On foot, you mean? Too far, the nearest place is a good sixty miles away, and it is rough country."

"Where exactly, are we?"

"Thomas Lake. About a hundred and twenty miles north-east of where we picked you up."

Knocked me down, you mean, I thought.

"Don't you have some kind of signalling device on the plane, which makes it easier to find you if you crash?"

He shook his head.

"Come on," I said, slipping my hands under Hank's armpits. "Grab his feet, let's get him down beside the lake, might help to get some water on his face. At least you can clean up that gash."

We carried him between us, and laid him down in the shade of the trees bordering the lake. I left Don to sponge his face.

Aubrey gave me a questioning look, as I dropped back into the seat beside him.

"Not good." I summarised; then gave him a general report on the condition of Hank, and the essence of the conversation with his brother Don.

We sat a while, discussing the situation, arriving back where we'd started...stuck; with no answers. Like all pointless conversations, it remained so, leaving us mentally twiddling our thumbs.

A period of silence prevailed, pregnant for my part, with conflicting thoughts. However, Aubrey proved to be one of those who seem unable to sit for long and keep their mouths shut.

"Can you drive a car Harry?"

They say something, anything; for want of something to say, doesn't matter that it's out of context. Their mouths operate independently from the brain. Anything can spout out. I find, from observation, that their words are invariably arranged to form a question. They work you into a position where you either have to answer, or appear rude.

I debated whether I should answer this time.

"Of course," I replied. "I drive a Bentley."

Low profile, of course, it's not done to brag, all right to toss it out though, in answer to a direct question. If he wants a game of one-upmanship on this one I thought…let's play. Guns no, cars and bikes; I've got the ammunition.

"I suppose you drive quite well?" he asked, irritatingly unimpressed.

"I think I can hold my own," I conceded starchily. I wondered if the old buffer was going to offer me a chauffeur's job. While I was formulating the words, to cut him to the quick, he went on…

"Then I think you could fly this plane out of here," he said.

Which left me sucking air…"You've gone completely bloody mad?" I almost shrieked at the fearful implications of his outrageous suggestion.

"Calm down, my boy, easy," he said in a syrupy voice. "Look at this dash-board, it's almost exactly like one in a car." He'd have made one hell of a car salesman. "See, this is the ignition, with a key conveniently in it. This figure of eight wheel arrangement, I bet that makes it go up, or down, and probably tilts it sideways too. A pedal for each foot, I expect they'd be for turning; work the rudder. It's even got the same dials, see, one for petrol another for oil pressure; printed right on them." His finger was busy as a pointer. "This ones for speed, and I'll take a guess; this knob is the accelerator. Best of all, there's the compass; no road map required."

I interrupted his sales pitch. "Hold it, just hold it. What you have conveniently forgotten to mention, is all these other dials and switches, any one of which could trigger the self-destruct system. So let me just scuttle your idiotic fantasy with these words…Piss off." And I felt I handled it with remarkable restraint, more so, as I was almost panting in horror.

"Just try it," he went on smoothly, holding up a hand to ward off further obscenities. "Drive it about a bit, that's all I'm saying, get the feel of it. What's the harm in that? At the very least, we get to boat around the lake. Never know; we might find some sign of a presence."

CHAPTER THIRTEEN

It took some swallowing, but I finally digested his alternate suggestion. He did have a point. It certainly wouldn't hurt to take a look at the perimeter of the lake. After all, we only had Don's say so, that the place was deserted, and I still thought he looked crafty.

If I ignored the wings on the plane, it was just a boat. Twin hulled, with a propeller. I could live with that. Get the thing started then try puttering about. Spy out the land round the lake, by which time Hank might be sitting up and taking notice.

With those guidelines firmly established, I allowed my eyes to rove over the various dials and controls. Had to admit there was a similarity, as far as the instruments were concerned, with those in a car. I tried to recall what I knew about the way aircraft are controlled. Sum total of which; wasn't worth adding up. First things first, how do I start it? There was a key in a switch, a tricky looking gizmo with four positions. Experimenting, I turned the key to the first position; which was marked MAG 1, whatever that meant-not much…nothing happened. Nothing suited me fine. I tried the next position, only because Aubrey sat there, eyeballing my every move, and missing nothing. This position was labelled MAG 2, twice as much of whatever? Nothing happened there either. I turned the key to MAG B, and got sweet Fanny Adams.

Aubrey leaned across. "Maybe you should be pressing this button as well Harry."

I gave him a haughty look, which clearly said, 'Don't muck about with the pilot mate', and pressed the button. A grinding noise commenced, the engine coughed a puff of smoke from its housing; then with a roar…it started.

Hurriedly reaching for the red Ping-Pong ball protruding from the dash panel, to check if it was the throttle, I gave it a push. It was. The increase in engine speed, resulted in the plane taking a run at the beach. I quickly pulled the throttle out again, and turned the key back to off.

Turning to Aubrey, who was visibly bouncing in his seat like a kid at a circus and smiling broadly, "Oh, bloody bad luck," I said. "Too bad we crashed."

"Crashed? Nonsense; just ran aground. Start it up again, and stick it in reverse," he suggested.

"Planes don't go backwards."

"Ah…yes, I see. We'll shove it backwards then, by hand. Turn it round too, then you can have another go, you're doing just splendidly Harry. Come on, we'll soon have you underway again."

What can you do with an idiot? As he opened the door and climbed out, I followed him.

Don was at the water's edge as we stepped off the float. "What the hell's going on?" he wanted to know.

Aubrey, apparently in charge of the shore-party, answered. "We intend to take our plane out, for a turn round the lake. Lend a hand young man and push on this float with me. Harry's bigger he can manage the other one on his own. We'd like it back in the water and turned round."

You saying, one of you can fly it?"

"I can't," said Aubrey. "But Harry is learning; he'll have it off in no time. Be a good chap now, we'll all push together."

Don looked at me, oddly, to say the least. "Is he kidding?"

"Yeah, he's one great kidder," I agreed. There was no way this Harry planned to "have it off."

Aubrey in the meantime was casting a knowing eye at the task in hand. He issued directions, had us applying muscle on his command of "Heave," and the joint effort concluded with the plane afloat, pointing in the right direction too, away from the shore.

Leaving Don standing on the beach, looking slightly bewildered and panting, with instructions from Aubrey to revive his brother, we waded out and dripped our way back to the seats. Re-starting the engine, this time with a confident flourish I eased the throttle in, this time with caution. The engine revs increased, the propeller spun faster, the plane moved. It crept away from the shore, decided not to head out onto the lake, and took a curving course back towards the shore. I remembered the pedals, put my feet on them, did a little dance, and the plane responded by obeying my feet. With me in control we headed for the open expanse of the lake.

With plenty of water around us, I boned up on the pedals, and managed to get the hang of it after a few erratic turns. Feeling I was reasonably competent, after executing a figure-of-eight turn, I steered the plane closer to the shore. Then we commenced an inspection of the shoreline. I took us in a clockwise direction; for some reason I was better at right turns.

Concentrating on the steering, I left the searching to Aubrey.

Don was right. The search turned out to be fruitless. Naturalists would think this place was heaven....not a trace of humanity. Aubrey and I, had we found it to be polluted by civilisation, would have been equally ecstatic.

Every mile of the long irregular perimeter had been scrutinised by Aubrey before we arrived back within sight of our starting point. By which time, I felt like the Red Baron, having acquired a fair amount of expertise in the art of steering.

My confidence was growing. I even began to tease myself with the fantasy that actually flying the plane was really no big deal. After all, I said to myself; getting airborne simply meant doing what I was doing now-only faster. Common sense really, if I belted along fast enough, the wings would do their stuff, and off we'd go...off into the wild blue yonder. Looking at the far end of the lake, and the blue yonder above it, it looked like it just might be possible. The land at that end of the lake was flat; apart from the trees, looked as though it was made for a take-off. Providing a chap could clear the trees?

What about turning...in the right direction after I get up there, I wondered? Well, the pedals should work the same. The wind going past the rudder; made it turn on the water, it should work in the air. May have to bank the plane a touch; do that with the wheel. Not too much or I'd find myself upside down. The hairs on the back of my neck started to act up again.

I wouldn't know how fast to fly, to keep the thing in the air. Yes I would; whatever speed it left the water at, would be its flying speed. Have to make a note of that at take-off. That speed would be the minimum, anything over, and the plane should stay up there.

Very good Harry...now let's see you get it down again? Would come down all right; any false move on my part would do that. The thing is how to accomplish it in one piece? I suppose, if I could find a long enough stretch of water, I could simply drive it down. By slowly losing height, until the floats touched the water, then cutting the throttle and coasting to a stop.

"I think you could do it Harry," said the voice of doom beside me. It was Aubrey.

"No I couldn't. I've been thinking about it. Can't be done, we'd come a hell of a cropper. I prefer to die some other way."

"We won't come any cropper you're getting better all the time. Taken us round the lake a treat. Practice a bit longer. Try a couple of faster runs, get the feel of it; see how it behaves at speed."

Not a bad idea I thought, doing a couple of fast gallops up and down the lake. Waste a bit more time; might be fun, and surely Hank would recover soon.

"Fair enough," I agreed. I turned the plane, heading out from the shore again, taxiing quite expertly now. Positioning the plane so that we were looking up the length of the lake, with the distant shore centred in the windscreen. I pushed in the throttle and we surged forward.

"You watch this dial," I told Aubrey, tapping the speed indicator. "Keep me informed of the speed."

As our pace increased, he dutifully started to intone, "Ten...Twenty...Thirty..."

I wondered how much speed I could risk. I quickly calculated, the plane being roughly the same weight as a small car, probably eighty miles an hour.

As Aubrey continued his chant, "Forty...Fifty..." the pauses getting shorter, the plane began to feel as though it was getting on top of the water. I eased forward on the wheel, to discourage any silly thoughts it might be having about going flying. If felt like I was driving a speedboat that had dragged itself up, and was skimming the surface.

We had lots of lake in front of us; this was feeling good, so I kept her going. The water ahead of us, looked to be slightly ruffled, I wondered how the floats would react to the slight chop.

Suddenly things changed. With a little bounce, we were off the water. Bloody hell; we were climbing!

My first reaction, which understandable wasn't fast, was to yank the throttle knob out. A quick look down changed my mind. It was too far to drop. I looked ahead again; the trees were too close. Up was safer. I gave the throttle a shove instead of a yank. Gently, oh so gently; and with the trepidation of a virgin when she's faced with the real thing, I eased the stick towards me.

The rate of climb increased, along with my pulse. Remarkably, all seemed to be under control...as far as the plane was concerned. I was scared to twitch a muscle, much less move, for fear of disturbing the plane's agreeable attitude. It was doing fine on its own.

I chanced a quick look down. The trees I'd worried about; those on the far shore of the lake were passing a long way below us. We had cleared them all right...I shuddered when I saw how many hundreds of feet we were above them.

"By God Harry, you've damned well done it," Aubrey was shouting. "Bloody good show," he roared.

131

Silly sod, I hadn't done a thing. It had just happened. I was too mesmerised by the events though, to make any comment disclaiming responsibility. I sat quite still, frozen in time, space, and chair.

I stayed in that condition, mainly staring at the altitude dial. I watched the hand slowly edge its way round, until it passed the two thousand feet mark. I'd been deferring the decision to do something about it, for the last thousand feet. I had to do something about stopping the climb. Level off? Move the wheel forward you clot, easier said than done; I hated to move anything. I forced myself. So, gently teasing the wheel little by little away from me, while watching the altitude reading slow its climbing rate, until it stopped, I allowed the wheel to come back towards me, and treated myself to sigh of relief when the hand on the dial confirmed a constant height was being maintained.

What to do next? We're up, we're flying level; but where do we want to go? I looked at the compass; it said we were heading west. I remembered Don saying the lake was Northeast of where they had picked me up. The opposite of Northeast, was Southwest, so if I could coax the plane; that was the direction to point it in. Where they'd picked me up, lay the sea. If I had any hope of getting the plane down, the open sea might just be big enough to accommodate my approach.

Right you are then, I had to make a turn. Get the compass needle, pointing from where it was now to south-west. Not much of a turn; a bit to the left. Try the left peddle? Lean the wheel to the left? Which one or a touch of both? The last seemed right to me, so they both got a touch. It worked, if my lips had been loose enough, I would have smiled. A perfectly delightful slow turn, which I held when the needle on the compass assured me, we were heading south-west; spot on.

I was actually flying the thing! My commands were being obeyed. I must have been born to fly. The old confidence was beginning to bubble. I was in charge!

"Be a good idea, to go up a trifle." That was my second officer, Sir Aubrey Bexley, no less.

In my new role of commander, I felt brave enough to peel my eyes away from the dashboard to find out what the lad was on about. He was shoving his digit finger around, alternating between up and in front of us. I couldn't see far up, so I looked forward. The ragged line, of a range of mountains, was rearing their ugly heads along the horizon ahead.

Bastards; who the hell put them there? "How high, would you say?" I shouted at Aubrey.

"Higher, than we are."

Big bloody help! I looked at the speedometer; quite surprised, when I saw it registered a little over a hundred miles an hour. Well we took off at about seventy, so I decided I could chance a climb at a rate that kept our speed above that.

Easing the wheel back towards me, gently again, we commenced to climb. I juggled the wheel when the speed dropped back to eighty, which left us I felt a margin of safety.

I kept my eyes glued to the altitude meter again. I refused to look at the mountains, just that hand, creeping around the dial.

When Aubrey shouted, "Well done Harry, you missed them." The needle had reached six thousand feet.

I looked in front of us…the mountains had gone. Stretching ahead of us, on this sparklingly clear day, I could see a vista of undulating hills. Gradually diminishing in height to merge with what could only be the sea in the far distance. I wished I could sit back, and enjoy the view, but a new worry was already getting its teeth into my mind.

The worry of getting down and on that distant sea, I knew I had to do it gradually. No power dives thank you very much. Nothing else for it, it had to be gradual, but I desperately wanted to leave well enough alone. I'd managed to get us level again, naturally too; our speed was back to over a hundred. I knew, when I eased the wheel forward again, which I had to, to lose height, we'd start to go a lot faster than I was keen on. Nothing else for it; I had to move the throttle. But what came first? Move the wheel forward, or the throttle? Better too fast, than too slow? Too slow, and I'd drop, dead! Which quickly decided things…fast was best. Easing the wheel away from me, I watched the altitude inch down and the speed increase

133

dramatically. My hand went to the throttle. I pulled it back, smidgen by smidgen, trying to get the speed down around a hundred. Trial and error and a balance was finally achieved, between them, they did what I'd hoped for. We were back to my descending speed, eighty miles an hour.

I almost relaxed. I think I could have, if the problem of landing hadn't been hanging over my head; like the clappers of doom. But at least now, I had enough confidence to pay some attention to what lay ahead, and below.

The last of the hills were falling away behind us, the land below and ahead, flatter. Forests and lakes still predominating, but I could also see a large river.

Could it be the Fraser, which Vic the beachcomber had told me so much about last night? Was that only last night? If it was, we were on track. And the river, happily, was following the same course as the plane.

I wondered, not too seriously, if this might not be the place to try a landing. Then gave myself a reprieve, by deciding the river wasn't anywhere near long enough between curves, or anywhere near wide enough for that matter. 'Hang about,' I told myself. 'Head for the sea Harry, you'll need all that room.'

Naturally, as we were descending; the further we travelled, the lower we got. Indications of habitation were quite visible now; in fact it began to look too crowded, with an almost unbroken patchwork of fields.

At three thousand feet, we sailed over a town.

At two thousand, the river looked accommodating enough to tempt me…in places. But I was too high, much too high, with no desire to change anything, when I got lower, if a very long, very wide straight stretch turned up, then maybe.

At fifteen hundred feet, I came close to coming unstuck…a shattering experience. A commercial airliner overtook us, a giant shadow above and just to one side of us…Aubrey's side. He gave it a friendly wave; I nearly had kittens. What the flaming hell was he doing this low? It didn't take long to work that out we were on the approach to Vancouver International Airport.

It really was getting to be too much. Congestion I could do without. I needed space…air space. Those big planes wouldn't want to give it to me, and I didn't have the competence to get out of their way.

The game, already stacked against me, was acquiring the odds of Russian Roulette. One pull of the trigger remaining, nobody dead yet, and my turn next. It was obvious to me that our present course would take us over the airport, where the big boys would be barrelling around in droves, laying in wait to bat me out of the air.

I could change course? I'd done that once-I wasn't going to do it again. No, sod it; I was programmed for the long gentle approach. Not the least sure I could manage that, but I refused to consider any complicated additives.

At five hundred feet, I was confused. What to do? Go up? Level off? I did nothing.

Looking ahead, another problem lurked in the distance, a bridge crossing the river. Making me aware, like a kick in the balls, that the closer we got to Vancouver the more bridges we'd find spanning my river. The situation was growing desperate.

I reviewed the options. To get to the sea, (my first choice), I'd have to run the gauntlet of flying over the airport. If I waited much longer than about now, there'd be too many bridges to cross.

No decision needed. The choice was obvious. It was now. I looked down to see what I'd drawn. The stretch of river currently being offered (if I made up my mind fast) was reasonably straight, unobstructed, but much too narrow, and much too short.

Further on, was hell, this bit would have to do. Our landing place, or grave, had been selected. This is it, shit or bust, nothing more to think about.

Pushing the wheel away from me, the deed was done, I had committed us. We angled down. Too steep, how the hell did I know?

At fifty feet, and I didn't need the altitude meter to tell me, we were over our landing place. We were also going like a bat out of hell. I grabbed the red Ping-Pong ball, with the thought that I should pull it out slowly. Whether on impulse, or a desire to get both hands back on the wheel, I yanked it all the way out. The water was coming at me fast, I pulled the wheel towards me a trifle. We hit the water hard. We bounced back up. We hit the water again, I pulled the wheel back a lot.

We were coasting along, with our nose in the air. I couldn't see where we were going. Our speed dropped, as did the nose of the plane. I looked through the windscreen to see where we had finished up, or more accurately, where we had come down. We had stopped, with the engine still idling, in the middle of the river.

I let out a sigh, which came all the way up from my ankles.

CHAPTER FOURTEEN

We both sat, in wordless silence.

I offered a brief, but sincere, silent message of thanks to the Bloke who looks after such things.

Looking about us, at this wonderful world, this wonderfully kind river, this blessed sanctuary; I observed we were drifting up river. Both banks, together with the log booms tied to them, were slowly moving past the cockpit window.

Cocky with it now, I gave the engine a casual blip, while positively booting the rudder pedal. Very confidently, and fairly expertly, I directed the plane towards the booms on my side of the river.

Switching off, as the plane bumped alongside the booms, I flung open the door, hopped down onto the float, and stepped from there to the log boom. Yelling while in transit at Aubrey to find me something to tie us up with, I held the plane against the booms. The "something" he handed me as a mooring line, was the necktie he'd had his pants held up with.

It did the job, at a stretch-with nothing to spare. With the Chamber of Horrors secured, I flopped down across the logs, shut my eyes, and allowed an exquisite feeling of satisfaction to engulf me.

I lay, contemplating the wonderful complexity of human nature. The sheer blissful feathery comfort of the post-traumatic experience; the mind's reward endowed on those who have suffered the terrible stress of periods of dire peril.

"Thank you Harry. A most enjoyable trip, I must say." Garrulous Aubrey, who was squatting down beside me, was at it again. The man was unreal. How an innocent like him, has managed to survive all his years, boggled my mind. I have heard it said, "Where there is no sense, there is no feeling," a classic example was sitting right beside me.

"So glad you enjoyed it," I said wearily. "We do aim to please."

Reluctantly sitting up, shading my eyes with a hand, I surveyed the neighbourhood. My attention focused on a tug, coming up river towing a long snake of booms. A second, smaller tug, was fussing about at the tail-end.

"This could be where the publicity starts," I murmured, more to myself than him. "We should have a quick conference, some good stuff here, if we handle it sensibly."

"The only sensible way I want it handled," said Aubrey," is not to have any."

"No publicity? You're joking; I hope?"

"Not joking at all."

Bugger you! I thought. "Want to tell me why?" I said.

He fingered his chin, and as he gave me the piercing eye stare, he had that cranky look back in his eyes. "Let me just say this. I would prefer that there be no publicity." He pronounced the last sentence slowly and clearly. A more sensitive chap than myself might have detected a note of subtle menace in the tone.

"Might be hard to do," I pointed out, adding the same emphasis to my words, without trying to hide the challenge.

He stood up. I think he had the authoritative stance in mind. He lost it however, when he had to grab his pants to keep them up. He fired a couple of "Hrrmps" down at me, then, "I should of course, expect to make it worth your while. Hard work warrants appropriate rewards." He raised his eyebrows suggestively.

"That so," I replied, doing some hard, quick, thinking. You do when a bucket of cold water has been thrown at you. I'm sure the thought of all the publicity I could reap from this case was mainly responsible for the feeling of bliss I'd experienced a moment ago. If only clients could appreciate the value of publicity. In between that, I'm doing my rapid thinking.

I stood up. "Right, no publicity; if avoidable," I said briskly, tacking on the subject clause, in case I found a loophole. "So this is what we do. I'm going to hail those tugs, when they get up to us. Ask if I can use their radio, and charter another float-plane to fly back to the lake. One of us goes with it; to bring those two out."

Aubrey the instant volunteer! "That's me, I'll go. I was in a better position than you, to look around, in case the pilot chap doesn't know where it is."

"If it's on the map, and we got the Thomas Lake right, he'll find it." Might be better if I had him out of the way, I thought. "OK" I agreed. "But be sure you get to Don first, before whoever flies you in. Tell him, as far as you or I are concerned, there won't be any charges laid. That suit you?"

"Oh, yes, see what you mean. About the publicity you mean?"

"Right" I cut him short, the tugs were making good progress. "Explain to him, that there are a couple of conditions, in regard to us withholding charges. First, we are impounding the plane. The other is, they get it back on payment of…shall we say five thousand dollars, to cover our expenses?"

"Yes, hmm, yes, I suppose I could tell him that." He looked somewhat shook-up. But I hadn't the time to explain the facts of life to him.

"Good. I've just thought of another condition you can add. Tell him, we want all our belongings delivered to us, at the Regency, by noon tomorrow. And don't forget to add, between the conditions, that the alternative is jail. When you get back to this end, get the pilot to drop them off somewhere they can get an ambulance should that still be required."

"Just a minute Harry, don't you think what you've proposed, is pretty close to blackmail?"

"Could be, depends on your point of view. I prefer to think of it as just retribution. Talk about that later, time's up."

The lead tug was abreast of us. I started to wave my arms, pointing to the tug further back down the boom, then clenching my hand and holding it to my ear, a demented phone caller. I repeated this antic several times, polishing the performance as I went. It worked in the end. The helper tug detached itself from the tail of the boom, heading towards us. It swung past us, turned up current, and came to rest with its stern held against the boom by its idling engine.

A crew of two, one in the wheelhouse, and the other standing on the afterdeck, in answer to his query, I told him we had radio problems. A gesture invited me to use theirs. Explaining, that I was not familiar with their marine band, I asked if they would be kind enough to put out a call, for the salvage vessel Nocturnal Hooker.

One of them picked up the microphone and said into it, "Nocturnal Hooker—Nippy Yarder."

Almost immediately, a reply came back. "Nippy Yarder—Nocturnal Hooker." With which, I had the microphone handed to me.

"Vic? Harry Potts. I need picking up." Very apt, I thought; fair request to make to a hooker.

"Hi Harry. What is your location?"

I handed the microphone back to its owner, with a questioning look. He spoke some reference points into it, unintelligible to me, which Vic obviously understood, as his voice confirmed with a word. "Roger."

Asking for the microphone again, I pressed the button, and asked Vic how long before he would reach us.

"Half an hour"

"Roger," I told him.

Surrendering the microphone, I offered my thanks, which were cut short by a curt nod and a hand dropping pointedly to the throttle lever.

Getting the message, I hopped smartly off the afterdeck, stepping quickly back onto the boom. The tug was on its way before I could turn round. I watched as it surged back on station, and got back to the job of towing.

"Not too talkative were they," Aubrey contributed.

"Chasing the tide I expect. They know it won't wait for them. Did you get all that?"

"Vaguely, in half an hour eh, pretty damned quick, I'd say. Who is this chap Vic?"

We sat down on one of the bigger logs in the boom, and I told him how I'd hired Vic, a local beachcomber; as my backup...some insurance for my appointment at the jetty. Then, due to the premature attack on my person by the two we had abandoned at the lake, the insurance didn't pay off. But, things being the way they were, as he was publicity shy, it could in fact have been a smart move on my part. Because, the boat I had used, would probably have been salvaged by Vic. And unless he had panicked, which I doubted, he would still have it in a safe place. An abandoned boat would have raised a hue-and-cry, which would very quickly have put Sir Aubrey Bexley in the limelight. So, I pointed out, Vic's role was a bonus, which had only come about due to my diligent attention to detail. An item he, Aubrey, should remember to include, when he got down to totting up the appropriate rewards he had mentioned.

Aided by that constructive chatter, and a few other nudges on my part, time passed quickly. Most uncharacteristically of me to prattle away at a mile a minute, could have been nature hard at work, getting rid of the stress I'd accumulated during my brief career as a pilot.

In a way, I think it did me good. By the time Vic's boat came flashing up the river, I was feeling in good form.

"I was going to start worrying about you; anytime now." Vic said, as he tied his boat up.

"Sorry I wasn't able to keep you informed," I told him. "A minor setback, but everything's under control now. Can you charter me a plane? One like this," pointing to ours, "one with floats; now?"

"Sure. Where d'you want it, for how many passengers, and how far you want to go?" As he was talking, he was reaching through the sliding cabin window for the radio.

I gave him the information he'd asked for, which he passed on to a charter company. "Be here shortly," he said turning to me. "What's the problem with this one?" cocking his thumb at ours. "That the one you took off in?"

"Yes it is. Right now, there is a problem with its radio, among other things. I'd like you to tow it to a safe place somewhere an eye can be kept on it, until such time, I authorise its release. We'll expect a bill for the services, of course." I looked at Aubrey, "Right?"

"Oh absolutely"

"I'll take care of it then," said Vic, "no problem. Go aboard," he added. "No sense in standing out here log rolling."

After the three of us had stepped over the gunwale and onto the open aft cockpit, I introduced the two to each other.

"Vic, I'd like you to meet an associate of mine, Aubrey." They shook hands, exchanging the usual guff.

"You guys like a drink?" Vic invited.

We both almost simultaneously accepted. I couldn't speak for Aubrey, but I needed that drink. Alcoholic beverages are purported to be at their peek of desirability, following events that result in an unexpected extension of ones life expectancy. As far as I was concerned, I qualified.

Seemed like a good time to light up a cigar, which triggered another thought.

"Excuse me," I murmured. Scampering back over the side onto the boom and making a beeline for the plane, I clambered in and began to rummage. I found my cigar case tucked under one of the rear seats.

I rejoined my shipmates, with a stogie stuck in my face at a very jaunty angle.

Drinks had been poured. Bourbon, from a bottle labelled Southern Comfort. Neat; in mugs.

Ah the contentment. The aroma of cigar smoke, drinks liberally replenished as fast as they were downed…the companionship of stout hearted fellows.

Conversation flowed, like the drinks. Vic informed us we had landed close to a place by the name of Port Hammond. The Regency Hotel was a mere fifteen miles down the river. We were on the Fraser River.

He also filled us in on his activities last night at the jetty, telling us how he'd been tied up, on the other side of the jetty, actually sitting on it, watching my boat. He'd seen the plane land, come alongside me, then shortly afterwards take off. I hadn't flashed him, but after the plane had taken off he noticed my boat adrift. Thinking he'd better investigate, he went out to find out what was happening. Very surprised, he was, to find the boat abandoned, but decided; maybe that's why I hired him, in case I had to go off in the plane. He'd towed the boat back to the marina, told them I'd gone off with friends.

I congratulated him on his initiative in handling the matter. When he inquired what we and the plane was doing in this location, and why we needed to charter another plane. I patched together another story.

It went like this. I told him Aubrey was a developer, with interest in acquiring certain lakeside property. I, as his advisor, had wanted a first hand look at the property, before the deal was finalised. But, I stressed, it had to be at the right moment in the negotiations. But he, Vic, would understand how critical that was? He gave a knowing nod, indicating he knew all right.

Then he would also understand, I suggested, the necessity for secrecy. Other negotiations, with rival investors, required some tricky footwork. Another knowing nod indicated he could well see that too.

A terribly unfortunate mishap had occurred, I related, when the company pilot had taken a nasty fall, striking his head on a log. An event, subsequently, which had meant Aubrey and I having to fly the plane out. Neither one of us being too familiar with the area, we landed at the first convenient spot; then called him.

The impounding of the plane, yes, well, a question of liability really I explained. Tricky business, liability, I told him. In business, one should, as he probably appreciated, always avoid crippling court cases, if possible.

I told him Aubrey would be accompanying the rescue flight, while I would give Vic a hand in towing the plane to wherever he felt it would be in good hands. Then if he had the time, he could run me back to the marina.

"So there you have it," I said.

"The way it goes," agreed Vic, "win some…lose some."

Aubrey remarked that I narrated the circumstances, unbelievably well.

Vic said he hoped the deal worked out all right for us.

I assured him, that although things had looked a bit dicey at times, we both now felt a satisfactory conclusion was most likely.

The roar of our arriving charter plane brought us out of the cabin, thankfully taking the heat off my powers of imagination.

Aubrey, with his departure imminent, announced he was peckish. Vic rose to the occasion, by opening a can of pork-and-beans. Shoving a fork in it, I reminded Aubrey that time was money as far as the charter plane was concerned-his money. So he didn't hang about.

He sat looking out of the window as the plane moved off, forking beans into his mouth. We gave him a wave as he raised the fork in salute.

I watched the take-off with professional interest, thinking mine could have looked just as good. I wondered what Don had thought when Aubrey and I had taken off from the lake in their plane

I decided that it would have been worth a few bob, to have seen his face when it did.

While I had been watching this plane disappear from view, Vic had been busy laying out lines and shackles to the two floats of the plane. In no time, we were underway down the river, with my erstwhile wings following obediently behind us.

Relieving Vic at the wheel for a while allowed him to produce victuals for me. My beans were served hot, on a plate. With fork and knife provided…with coffee that would have sobered up a judge.

We were bucking the tide, Vic said. I could see the scenery wasn't exactly flashing past. Another hour, he figured, before we could drop the tow off in a safe place.

Enough time, I decided, for a nap. I asked Vic if he minded. He answered by clearing the clutter from the sole berth in the cabin. One sweep of his arm did it.

There wasn't much room to toss and turn, but it felt good, just to lay back. My mind started to flit over recent events, but it didn't get too far.

A couple of full-blown jaw stretching yawns convinced me that I really was tired. Couldn't think why? I wondered if it was the after effects of whatever had been used to keep me blacked-out last night. It had to have been more than the crack on the head. A rub with my hand confirmed that it hadn't been much of a crack. It wouldn't have put me out that long. Maybe they'd given me a whiff of chloroform? That might explain the reason for my ungentle manly conduct, in spewing over Aubrey's shoes this morning.

Funny case this turned out to be I got to thinking. Some highly suspicious aspects…the next thing I knew, Vic was shaking me, to lend a hand in tying up the plane to a dock.

He'd decided a spare berth at a tugboat company's dock was a safe place. We tied the plane up to his satisfaction. I retrieved the key, and locked the door, while Vic slipped into the office to make arrangements.

Ten minutes fast running after we'd left the plane, and I stepped back on the float at the marina.

Back where I had started from last night.

The float-plane base, to which Aubrey would be returned, was no more than a mile from the Regency Hotel. I asked Vic if he would mind waiting there for him.

"No problem," Vic said.

"Thanks for your help today," I said in genuine gratitude. "We couldn't have managed without you."

"You're welcome," he replied.

CHAPTER FIFTEEN

Taking the time to call at the marina office before I left the dock, I informed them I would no longer require the charter boat. "No problem," was the response.

My wallet was where I'd left it, under the foam mattress of the vee-berth.

Calling back at the office to settle my account brought me, "Have a nice day, thanks for the business."

"You're welcome," I said, heading for the foot of the ramp.

Pulling myself up the steep slope of it by the handrails, I became aware of the splashing, and general chatter of activity coming from the swimming pool. I felt a little flutter of pleasure, as my eyes rose above the level of the riverbank; to see the bikini set sunbathing, sitting, diving, and bouncing their offerings…a swinging scene.

Good time to book a couple of swingers for this evening, I determined.

Wandering, among the brightly coloured sun-shaded tables; I

studied today's selection. As nice a display of scantily clad female anatomical blessings, as I'd seen in many a day.

This is for me, my lust told me; suggesting I take the lot. My experience told me, sadly; one was all I could handle, so I looked around for availability.

Picking up a chair, I headed for it, a girl, in a swimsuit; sitting alone at a table, an obvious choice.

"Mind if I join you?" I asked, "The other tables seem a bit crowded, which gives me the opportunity to presume." I plonked the chair down at the table, a positive gesture.

I liked what I could see above the table, and I wasn't looking at the salt and pepper pots. Brunette; the hair swept back in a short sporty cut. Tanned skin which I could see plenty of: brown eyes, surrounded by their own lashes; high cheekbones, dimples, olive complexion. Wide mouth, attractively handling an abundance of white slightly oversized teeth, without looking uncomfortable about it. Full breasted, which the swimsuit top appeared to have under control. The age of the complete package, I'd say, at a guess…thirty-tops. And if what lurked under the table, turned out to be a matching set of parts, she wasn't going to get any complaints from me.

She said, not sounding too sure about my arrival. "Er…no, I guess I don't mind."

"Extremely decent of you, not intruding am I? I mean; not expecting company, anything like that?" I thought I'd get that sorted out as quickly as possible. No sense in wasting my best lines, on a non-starter. She wasn't fast with an answer; so suitably encouraged, I pressed right along.

"Been doing a spot of boating and fishing," I said. "Terrific out there on the ocean today; glorious weather we're having, aren't we?" Guaranteed to draw a response, who can resist a comment on the weather?

"Well I'm from Los Angeles, California. I guess I'm enjoying it being a little cooler."

"Los Angeles, are you really, how interesting. I have most pleasant memories of your city." I entertained her with an amusing incident that had happened to me on a visit there, a story…offering nothing but credit to her hometown. By the time the waitress shimmied up, looking for drink orders, a slender bond was established. She allowed me the privilege of buying her a drink; often the perfect bonding agent in cementing a relationship.

Her name was Nancy, a schoolteacher on holiday, staying at the hotel, having arrived just this morning. She was planning on seeing something of Vancouver before going on to Victoria, on Vancouver Island.

"Have you done Stanley Park yet?" I asked.

"No, I'm fresh off the plane, barely had time to unpack yet. Heard plenty about your famous park though, maybe I'll start off there tomorrow."

"It isn't my park, actually. From England myself; here for the odd day or two on business, don't you know."

She laughed; huskily; sexy. "You couldn't be anything else, but British. You talk like David Niven."

I wondered if some indication of kinship might help my cause—third cousin, or something.

"Know the lad well, he would approve of my sitting here flirting with Nancy," was what I settled for.

"Is that what you're doing?" she laughed.

"Of course," I laughed with her. Get in there Morton!…I was in.

It was plain sailing after that. We chatted over the drink; she agreed to go see the park with me tomorrow. Using that as a stepping stone, I proposed that possibility of us getting together this evening.

No violent objections were raised, so before excusing myself to go and get cleaned up I promised to call her later.

The day was getting better by the hour, I decided, as I headed into the hotel. A teacher, she'd said. Well, as long as I chose the subject, I was in the market for a lesson or two.

While picking up my key at the desk, I booked a room for Sir Aubrey Bexley; then headed for my room.

Eyeballing the phone on my bedside table as I peeled my clothes off, I debated calling Lady Helen. I should let her know Aubrey was all right. However, I decided that as Aubrey would be here shortly; it would be nicer if he made the call himself.

Strange thing…he had never once mentioned his wife to me, or even enquired about her well being. Not a thing. Funny bugger, I thought. Maybe he didn't think it the done thing, to discuss his wife with the hired help? I thought back to when we'd met, after I'd bronzed his shoes. I imagined if I'd allowed it, he would have been happy to keep our relationship on a squire-and-serf basis, although, he had come through when the chips were down. Still…it was odd.

I had a chuckle, more of a snicker really; when I pictured him arriving at the desk downstairs to book a room. No money, credit cards, or ID; and looking like a derelict. Perhaps I shouldn't have paved the way for him. He'd have pulled it off anyway; he has that air of confidence and authority that only good schools and rank can buy.

Ready to step into the shower, I looked at the phone again. I'm human. I wanted to share my triumph with somebody, anybody; even Chalky would do.

The idea of calling him in the early hours of the morning added some incentive. He's done it to me in the past, often just to crow over some tricky problem he's solved with some gizmo on his bloody locomotive. A few of those late calls had come at a most inconvenient time. Just what you need, when you're breathing heavy in a girl's ear and the bedside phone rings. And it's Chalky going on about a connecting rod, or something equally stupid.

Anticipating the pleasure of hearing his reaction to my success, I got on with making the call. He sounded chirpy when he answered. I hadn't awakened him-which was disappointing. Working late on his locomotive; evidently the climax of completion was imminent. So I got to hear about that…at my expense. Had he been paying for the call, I'd have got two words out of him; one of those would have been good-bye.

I bulldozed my way in, finally. "Success Chalky, I have rescued Sir Aubrey; he's safe and sound, and so am I."

"That's good. Another case bites the dust then."

Not a word of curiosity, the rotten sod. "What developments at your end?" I asked resignedly. "Find the bug?"

"No bug. That's the word from the experts. Water under the bridge anyway; case closed. So when are you heading back this way?"

"Not sure yet, what's the weather doing?"

"Cats and dogs."

"Might drag my heels a bit then; pick up a tan while I'm here. Give you a buzz when I'm coming. You might feel like a drive up to meet me."

"I might. Don't get sunstroke then."

"Don't get your feet wet," I remarked.

"Ta-ra."

I hung up. No good saying I didn't feel let down, because I did.

A shower and a shave later, I'd pretty well forgiven him. Sorting out; what I had in the way of casual clobber, I hung the most presentable on my freshly laundered body. Then pulling a chair up to the window, I enjoyed a cigar while keeping a lookout for the return of Aubrey in Vic's boat.

Well over an hour passed before Nocturnal Hooker hove into sight. A peaceful, yet thoughtful interlude it was too. I stubbed out my smoke and took the elevator down to the lobby.

Aubrey was standing at the desk when I got there and getting the...no-sir-yes-sir, three-bags-full-sir, routine.

"Ah, Sir Aubrey," I said formally. "Good trip, I trust?"

He turned to the sound of my voice. "Hello Harry. Yes, very successful, couldn't be better. He put his hand on my shoulder, giving me a shake, "Let's talk. Where's the bar?"

"Want to get cleaned up first?"

"I do, but it can wait. Get your priorities straight; lead me to the bar."

I led the way.

The bar was quiet; it was also dark. Dim lights are the norm in the cocktail bars of North America. A throwback I think to the days of prohibition, when to drink in the dark was the smart thing to do. Whatever the reason, one almost has to strike a match to see what you're drinking.

We groped our way to a corner table, where Aubrey got stuck into a dish of nuts.

Aubrey said, between chewing, "Well my boy, we can relax, the pilot chaps all right. Sitting up, and taking notice when we arrived back." Catching sight of a waiter sneaking about in the shadows, a good three tables away, he shouted, in a voice devoid of inhibitions, "Double scotch and ginger." His finger swung and pointed at me.

"Same." I told it.

It got pointed back to the waiter. "Make that two, at the gallop."

"How all right was the pilot?" I asked. "If you tell me he was fit to fly the plane, I'm going to go right off you."

He gave a guffaw; must have thought I was kidding. "Oh no, shouldn't think so. We had to help the poor blighter along. His senses were a bit vague, wasn't aware what was going on."

"What about the other business; talked to Don did you?"

"I take it you mean, your demands. Yes, I read him the riot act, laid down your conditions; in a pretty menacing tone too. He agreed, not happily; but he said he was grateful, in a way. Although, he thought you were a hard bastard Harry; quite convinced about that he was."

"The way the cookie crumbles," I remarked.

"Funny, he said something much the same."

With the drinks arriving, he busied himself trying to see how much ginger ale he was slopping into his scotch. "No good ordering a Whiskey Mac, on this side of the ocean Harry; don't know what you're talking about."

He got the mix to his satisfaction, raised his glass to me and offered, "Cheers Harry. Well done, and thank you very much."

"Cheers Aubrey, and thanks for the flying lessons." I chuckled.

We both began to laugh. Suddenly our experiences of the morning became hilarious. Odd things were remembered, which took on unaccountable humour. Things like, me telling Aubrey he stank; that really hit his funny bone. Me, reminding him of his nonchalant wave at the bloody great airliner which almost unhinged me.

We were on the second or third round, before a measure of

decorum returned. Even then, my having to buy the rounds, he found amusing. I didn't, but I couldn't help laughing. A thirsty knight; without the price of a drink, somehow tickled my warped sense of humour.

"So where did you drop the kidnappers off?" I asked, in an endeavour to bring us back to the present, and sanity.

"At the seaplane base; just a stone's throw down the river from here. Vic called a taxi, we helped load them in. Don said he was taking his brother to a hospital. Couldn't see the need myself; couple of aspirin, he'll be fit for duty."

"Bound to be," I said encouragingly, although doubting it. "To change to subject," I went on. "I imagine you'll be anxious to call your wife?"

The question seemed to take the levity out of him. He went quiet; I'd guessed right. Under that brusque facade, I thought, lurks a sensitive man.

He said though, albeit in a subdued voice, "No, that's not the way of it, I'm afraid. I'm not at all anxious."

I just looked at him, saying nothing. He moved his glass about the table, like an indecisive chess player. The condensation rings held his attention quite a while, before he spoke.

"A chap doesn't like to broadcast his personal affairs. However, I consider your involvement now, to be sufficient to deserve an explanation. Truth of the matter is, I'm divorcing my wife."

My reaction was, not surprisingly; that he had flipped; slipped a cog, or my ears were picking up another station. I had a clear three dimensional picture of the tear streaked caring wife, who had dispatched me with haste to retrieve her husband. A woman, whose deep concern for her husband's life, had shown so tragically in her sorrowful eyes.

"I'm sorry," I said.

"No need," he waved away my "sorry." "Had to happen, inevitable I suppose. Apparent to you, I'm sure; that Helen is quite a bit younger than I. Should never have married her, but there you are, no fool like an old fool. But you know the way it is, when one gets smitten with a woman."

I had no idea. I gave him a knowing look anyway.

"No sense or reason to it, is there? We simply have to have them." He added.

I wasn't going to deny that. Know the feeling well. Your brain hops between your legs, and points in the only direction it's willing to think. But surely, it's love from the heart that makes a marriage? My experience hasn't reached there yet, so I wasn't about to condemn the bloke for getting things mixed up. So I buttoned my lip.

Just as well…he hadn't finished yet. "I won't embarrass you with the sordid details. Sufficient to say, Helen was guilty of a gross indiscretion, in fact several. When sanity finally prevailed, I had her investigated. Disgusting evidence came to light, that was shortly before I left to come here. I told her then, that I would open divorce proceedings. I suggested she should clear out of the Hall, before I returned."

"I can see that you would," I said. Obviously, there were several pertinent questions I would have preferred to ask, but the timing would have been terrible.

"Exactly, only reason she married me was the title and the Hall. It's easy to be wise though, after the event, right. Nothing she can do about those now; after her behaviour, and the evidence it provided. I told her, she'll get nothing; and I'll make damned sure she doesn't. An actress you know, when I married her, and not a very good one at that. Gave her everything she asked for Harry, I suffered all her extravagances, seldom complaining. What I gave her is naturally hers to keep; but there it ends."

Not a good actress? After the performance she put on for me? Academy Award stuff, if ever I saw it. Maybe Chalky knows what he's talking about, when he complains that I'll believe anything a woman tells me. I think his actual words were, "You can't get your mind out of their knickers."

I called for another round. What I needed, was information. So many things were not gelling, so many interesting possibilities wriggled beneath the surface. I decided to grope, and see what I could see.

"Upsetting time, you've had," I probed, "with the kidnapping coming on top of your domestic problems. Have to put them both behind you now; get back to living."

"Pick up the threads eh? I shall. Already have, full speed ahead now; get back in the swing."

"Must have shaken," I almost said your wife, "er Helen? Knocked her for a loop I expect; getting the call, telling her you had been kidnapped."

"Took it in her stride, I should think."

"Bit of luck though, her still being there," I delved.

"Wouldn't have made the slightest difference, given the same call; my man Saunders, would have set the same wheels in motion. He'd have got on to Bill Rodgers; the key man in my business affairs. Which I'm sure, is precisely what Helen did."

"Bill Rodgers!" I exclaimed. "Yes, Helen mentioned it was he who suggested she call me, although she didn't go into details."

"Ah, I see." Whatever it was he saw, he found worth thinking about. "Then no doubt, you have done work for Bill in the past?"

"I'm not prepared to answer that Aubrey. 'Afraid you'll have to ask him."

"Good man Harry. Quite proper, I respect that."

While he was impressed with my integrity, I thought I'd dig deeper. "To go back to your domestic problem, you may wish to avail yourself of another of my services. I do offer a comprehensive range. For instance; you have only to reveal the name of the third party in the triangle, to arrange a drastic change in the gentleman's intentions."

He laughed; that infectious bellow. "It does appeal. I'll wager you could do it too. But no Harry, thank you all the same. I bear the chap no malice; perhaps I should reward him. No, I'm over that now. My enforced confinement gave me plenty of time to think. I can put it all in perspective now. I don't mind telling you the chap's name; don't think that it will come out in the wash anyway. Rowland Cooke with an e…poor blighter doesn't know what he's let himself in for. No, no malice from me, just my sympathy."

What d' you know, I mused. Rowland Cooke, the driver of the Morris the leading man in a dirty picture co-starring Helen the recently estranged wife of the victim.

"Very forgiving of you Aubrey, I must say." I said, with my mind otherwise engaged.

"It's easy; once you've put the whole thing behind you," he said stifling a yawn. "Excuse me; you know Harry, suddenly I'm tired, whacked. If you don't mind, I think I'll go and get my head down."

He could leave as soon as he liked, I needed thinking time now. "Yes," I encouraged, "you look knackered. Couple of hours will do you good. I'll stop by and give you a shout then, you'll be hungry by that time." I knew I would.

"Good man Harry." Already ambling off, as he said it.

Watching, as he made his way out of the bar, I wondered about him. As I didn't want another drink, and the gloom of the bar was making me feel like a mole, I left.

The place for constructive thinking, I made up my mind, was out in the fresh air. Not by the pool, too many distractions; perhaps, a secluded spot on the river bank.

Then, as I moved through the lobby and spotted the coffee shop, I realised I was hungry. And I can't think on an empty stomach. So I changed course, found a quiet corner in the eatery, and ordered a snack. The place was almost deserted, just what I needed for a spot of heavy thinking, so I got the old grey matter into high gear.

By the time I'd finished my apple pie with ice cream, I had everything worked out. My mind quickly grasped the almost complete picture, deftly slotting the pieces into place.

This is the way I figured it. Here's this bloke Rowland Cooke, who's having it off with her Ladyship...and jolly good luck to him. Been in like Flynn myself; given any encouragement. Aubrey, the squire, smells a rat as husbands will, if they're not too busy having it off with someone else. So, off he goes to the neighbourhood private-eye, Peeping Tom, the snapper of compromising positions. Tom does his stuff; gets some good shots of hitherto private parts, with faces to match, and delivers same to Aubrey. Whereupon Aubrey with his eyes opened wide now, gives Humpin' Helen the old heave-ho. Now poor old Rowland—who probably is without two pennies to rub together, is about to get stuck with penniless Helen. But Rowland; having a drink at his local one day, sobs his heart out to his good friend, Peter Hepworth. Now Peter, as has been shown; is a very devious chap, and not backward when it comes to raising illegal funds. He comes up with the kidnapping plan. Helen has only to pretend she gets the ransom call. She then gets the ball rolling by contacting the keeper of the loot, who is not about to let Aubrey cool his heels in confinement. Enter the berk, me, to deliver the diamonds. Except I was supposed to hand them over to the first bloke who asked for them; like Peter Hepworth, which would have given the departing couple, Rowland and Helen, a pension fund to count as they walked hand in hand over the horizon. Not to mention, a chunk for Peter the director.

Well, with all revealed to me, a lot of other things began to make some sense. Aubrey was coming to Canada anyway, and I'll bet Peter just happened to have a couple of friends here, Hank and Don. And who would be suspicious of the trio, safely smacking their lips in England?

And of course they knew when I took possession of the diamonds…they knew when I was coming to collect them. Helen, I remember, was convincingly insistent that I take them with me then; little wonder a bug wasn't necessary on the phone line.

Naturally too, they had to have a Muggins like me. Made it all appear to be so authentic.

What about the attempt though, to get rid of me when they got rid of Aubrey? Good idea. Things had gone wrong though, they didn't have the ransom. With Aubrey and myself doing a disappearing act, they couldn't get the blame. Helen would report the facts to the police, in due course, telling them how I had set off with the ransom. Bill Rodgers, the keeper of the loot, would confirm that.

If I hadn't put a spoke in the wheel, or rather the Bentley into the Morris, by not handing over the diamonds they'd have got away with it. No wonder Peter was so keen on doing a deal with me.

That's it, I decided. Had to be the way it was; everything fits. All right, so the bits fit. What to do about it?

Nothing; is what I do about it. Its one thing to figure out a plot, but another thing to prove it, did I want to? Any profit in it? Two no's in a row pretty well resolved the quandary.

Reviewing the positive aspects: Aubrey survived the diamonds were safe. I survived. The thing was, as things stood, would my fee survive? When all was said and done, the only remuneration I had received from Helen, apart from expenses, which Aubrey was spending like a drunken sailor, was a verbal agreement to cough up three thousand—when the ransom had been delivered. That clause alone would sink me. And on the basis of my theory, Helen's credit rating was batting zero.

A situation, which as I spelled it out to myself, had the old heart palpitating. Steady Harry, stay cool. In the moment of calm that prevailed, I decided to hit Aubrey with my bill over dinner tonight.

CHAPTER SIXTEEN

Taking a stroll, after leaving the coffee shop, I interrogated my brilliant theory with enough searching questions to tear it to shreds. It stood the strain.

By the time I'd wandered the riverbank in a storm of thinking, in both directions from the hotel, I considered Aubrey to have used up his two hour nap period.

So I zeroed in on his room door, and gave it a good battering. Surprisingly, the door opened almost immediately, presenting a framed picture of Aubrey wearing a towel round his middle.

"Thought you said you were tired," I remarked.

"Had a catnap—enough to charge my batteries, I think the shower did me the most good. It woke me up enough to make a few phone calls. Do you realise, I've nothing to wear?"

"Phoning your tailor were you?"

"Ha, ha, very funny old chap. Damned inconvenient though, can't say I'm very anxious to climb into this tacky stuff again." He took a kick at his old clothes, which were heaped in a pile on the floor.

"Be a devil; live dangerously-one more time," I told him, "then we'll beetle off and get you fixed up with new stuff."

He shrugged his shoulders. "Suppose I'll have to; not much choice. Certainly not staying cooped up here, 'til my bags get returned."

While he, with nose turned up, began putting the old clothes on, I phoned for a cab.

The cab dropped us off at the nearest department store, where a transformation to North American style attire took place, though not without some ungracious bitching on Aubrey's part. He didn't even know his size. I don't even think he knew you could buy clothes off the rack. Must be handy, having "my man" to handle these minor irritations. Funny thing, I contemplated, as he paraded the new ensemble for my approval—Aubrey made the clothes look good.

Leaving the department store, and wandering through the Mall complex, we agreed on one of the many restaurants, and tried our luck.

A family restaurant, tarted up as a fast food joint. But a good appetite makes a banquet of almost anything. We devoured our dinner with gusto. Then settled back with our coffee; both of us comfortably at home behind one of the cigars he had selected on our walk through the mall.

Down to business, I thought. Pulling the bag of diamonds out of my pocket, I placed it with a degree of melodrama on the table in front of him.

"Aubrey," I said. "I've clothed you, fed you, and apart from needing a shave, you look in first class condition. I consider I've returned you; almost as good as new. I hereby relinquish my commitment. That little bag is a bonus for you."

"What do you think it will look like?"

"What?"

"A beard," he was rubbing his chin. "Thought it might be an excellent time to grow one; got about a ten day start."

"Anything could be an improvement." I said.

He chuckled. "Glad to be rid of me are you Harry?"

I had to grin back at him; it's hard to stay mad at a nut-case. "Nah, not really, I'm just getting used to you actually."

He laughed, and took a puff on his cigar, contentedly blowing smoke signals up over our heads. Rolling the cigar in his fingers, he focused on my eyes. "Harry, I want to tell you a few things. First, I'd like you to know it has been a pleasure meeting you and spending time with you. I mean that sincerely. I'd like to presume that you and I are at the beginning of a long friendship. I am aware...and not because you told me earlier today in no uncertain words, that what you do is a business, in which I am a client."

He waved away my attempt to interject. "Let me finish. One of the phone calls I made earlier went to Bill Rodgers; you know who he is. Mainly, the call was to let him know I was back in the saddle. But also, I wished to know the financial arrangement between you and me. Incidentally; the fee you agreed to was on Bill's recommendation. Obviously, you have done more than fulfilled your commission." He gave the bag of diamonds a poke with a finger. "The very fact, that this is here, suggests a great deal of dedication on your part. I intend to reward you for that. A customary finder's fee, for merchandise of this nature," tapping the bag to make the point, "is ten percent of the appraised value, which means I owe you...probably fifty thousand dollars U.S. Plus three thousand pounds for delivery of the ransom. To whom, my enquiries revealed—was not specified. However, and this is something I picked up from you today...I'm going to throw in a small condition. Which is; you take these diamonds back to England when you go. Is that acceptable Harry?"

"No problem," I said, trying to keep my face together, "consider it done. As to the fee, and your complimentary words, I don't quite know what to say."

"Say nothing. Put these stones back in your pocket. And those are the last words, as a client that I intend to say." Reaching across the table, he offered me his hand. "Friends from now on Harry?"

"Friends, Aubrey," I agreed as we shook hands warmly.

I felt a bit second-hand really, as I remembered my earlier thoughts about hitting him with my bill at dinner. His generosity had floored me. The figures had me in ecstasy. His words had touched me.

We didn't dally after that, even so, it was well past ten o'clock when we arrived back at the hotel. Aubrey declined a visit to the bar, saying he felt now ready for a good night's sleep.

With a, "Carry on Harry," he dismissed me in the lobby, and took off in an elevator.

Buoyed by my good fortune, I felt ready for anything. On the off-chance I phoned Nancy's room. No reply. Too bad. Well I wasn't ready for bed…sleep-wise that is, so I thought a stroll around the marina might fill the bill. As I wandered back through the lounge towards the rear exit however, whom should I spy? None other than Nancy herself, she was sitting in a large overstuffed armchair, legs wastefully curled under her, thumbing through a magazine.

She looked positively stunning. In a white dress, off the shoulder I think the expression is, but describes it well anyway. The white accenting her golden tan splendidly, as good an ad, for a bit of the old slap and tickle, as I ever hope to see.

My pace picked up several notches as I strode towards her. "Hello Nancy, would you believe I just called you," throwing her a smile full of soft violins, cupids and roses, as I said it.

"Did you now; how was I?" She burbled, smiling.

Quick wit—I like that. "Ravishing," I replied. "You murmured…in a jolly sexy voice, I might add. That you madly desired to take a moonlight stroll with me beside the river."

"Did I? Well let me tell you buster, if I said it, you'd better believe it. We Nancy's follow through."

She uncurled out of the chair. I offered her my hand, to assist the operation. Contact established…I nurtured it. We left the lounge, hand in hand.

We bantered our way out and along the paved walk that followed the riverbank, her hand still in mine. The moon and the stars, joining forces with the coloured neon lighting festooning the buildings, created a profusion of reflections from the water.

Later, but not much, our arms resting on each others shoulders, we leaned against the pier railings, breathing the cedar scented night air, and watching the moving lights of passing boats.

Women lap this stuff up. I felt her arm slowly edging its way down to my waist. The romance associated with the aforementioned attractions works great.

Later, quite a lot, we chose my room. I thought it might be the gentlemanly thing to be host. Nancy wasn't a bit like that girl in Tunbridge Wells—couldn't recall her name at that moment. Nancy didn't believe in preliminaries like getting to know you better. Down to the buff and no messing about, Nancy was a very athletic female.

The night flew. Time does, when you're one of a pair of players…playing the games that lovers play.

Dawn was breaking too, when we broke it up. Nancy was donning her knickers and whatnots at about six. Blowing me kisses, as she let herself out.

Aubrey phoned at eight, wanting to know if I would care to join him for breakfast.

I wouldn't; but said I would, in half an hour.

Unthinking sod, I thought. Probably snored like a pig all night. Then remembering the generous finder's fee, I eased up on him. Wasn't his fault, I'd missed my sleep. Can't have it all ways, I decided.

I was almost awake, when I made my entrance for breakfast. Aubrey was at a window table, sipping orange juice and reading a newspaper. At another table, I spotted Nancy doing much the same thing—on her own.

Tricky situation, when only half your wits are at home. Not much else I could do though, I went to Nancy, exchanged smug smiles and asked her to join my friend and I. Then escorted her across to Aubrey's table, who as he saw us approach, rose courteously.

"'Morning Aubrey, I'd like you to meet Nancy. Nancy is on holiday from Los Angeles, we met yesterday on the patio. Nancy, allow me to introduce Sir Aubrey Bexley."

I saw the flush on her cheeks, and the glaze of her eyes, and diagnosed an acute case of the celebrity syndrome. She did a mock-up of a courtesy. He kissed the back of her hand, a display of smooth charm…old fashioned style.

Before I'd spooned the last of my cereal down, I was past-tense; a fading memory. Nancy appeared to be spellbound by Aubrey...or his bloody title, flashing toothy smiles like she was flogging toothpaste. While he was showing a smarmy side I would never have suspected.

As I commenced an assault on my bacon and eggs, she prattled on about her holiday. Sparing me a coy look from her peripheral vision, she told Aubrey that Harry had promised to take her to see Stanley Park today.

Aubrey, fairly fast off the mark for a rusty old seducer, told her how unfortunate it was that Harry wouldn't be available. It must have slipped Harry's mind, but Harry had an extremely important business meeting today. An exchange of property, he told her, which he was certain Harry wouldn't want to miss. But; by a frightfully opportune coincidence, he planned on visiting the park himself, this very day. He actually held and patted her hand, as he told her he would indeed be most honoured, to have her accompany him.

"I don't suppose you are aware my dear, but Lord Stanley, whose name the park bears...."

I switched off. What a load of cod's wallop. I wasn't taking notes on his routine. Take that title away; he'd have been hit by a rebuff that would have rattled his teeth.

Polishing off the last piece of toast I always save, to mop up egg spillage and other oddments, I concluded that as far as Athletic Nancy was concerned, Harry was a spent force. She had found a real Knight in shining amour. And God help the poor bugger, I thought, if he ever takes it off.

Nancy left first. She had to do something with her nose. I could have offered several suggestions.

Aubrey, leaning towards me confidentially, after Nancy left, "too slow Harry, way too slow. Young handsome well built young fellow like yourself should have swept her off her feet in a flash. Met her yesterday, you say? I can see I'll have to give you a crash course on how to dazzle the ladies. By the by...how are the expenses holding up?"

"If you're referring to my travelling expenses, they were holding up well; 'til you took a run at them."

"Never mind, let me have couple of hundred to cover the day. We'll square up later."

I counted them out; pushing them across to him. He picked up the breakfast tab, gave me a grin; and pushed it across to me. I looked at it. For three! He knew how to rub it in.

"Have a nice day," I managed, as he rose to his feet.

"Same to you," as he scuttled off he added, "See my bags up to the room when they arrive, will you old chap?"

Maybe the randy old bugger wasn't as old as he looked, I decided; probably won his wrinkles from loose living.

"More coffee," the waitress asked, as I made no effort to follow Aubrey.

"Why not," I agreed, with nowhere to dash off to in a hurry.

I sat, idly thumbing through Aubrey's discarded newspaper, alternately giving a thought to where I should invest the unexpected windfall from Aubrey and chatting up the waitress. A thoroughly pleasant girl, she turned out to be. Her name was Irene. Her hovering presence was tantalisingly opportune. After the piddling slurs cast by the Ancient Knight, on my ability to dazzle the ladies, I couldn't resist flashing the old charisma to see if it needed dusting off.

I gave her a couple of minute exposures, with my routine on high beam, seemed to be working all right. That is not to say she looked dazzled, or suffered any other impairment to her vision, or was even forced to shield her eyes. But, she was receptive to my suggestion that as she went off duty after the lunch trade, and that as I too had been wondering what to do for the afternoon, we could perhaps join forces to view the local sights.

With that decided, the desk paged me, and I made by my departure, "Till later then."

It was Don who waiting at the desk, and he was here for the express purpose of getting the plane out of hock. He wasn't sociable; I asked after his brother anyway. His brother was mad, he informed me. I said I was of the same opinion. It was lucky for me, Don told me, that he'd been able to keep Hank away from me. I said I'd rejoice, when I had a minute, and had he brought money"

We retired outside, Don and I, to a van in the parking lot. Aubrey's luggage was piled in the back.

Don began to slant the dialogue towards me having to settle for the luggage, without the money. I grabbed him by the hair and put a dent in the van with his head...that quickly put him back on track. With tears in his eyes (pulling hair does that) he spun me a sob story. The main theme being the tragedy of his life's savings being wiped out, by my excessive demand of five thousand dollars.

With my fingers playing over the dent in the side of the van, as a sort of sinister sound track, I gave him a heart-to-heart regarding the high cost of crime (to the perpetrator) versus the discomfort of confinement...then had him count the money out.

I whistled up the hall porter to carry Aubrey's bags up to his room, presented the key of the floatplane to Don, and wished him better luck with future ventures.

With the thought that maybe Vic would be around, I headed for the Marina. Feeling lucky, when I spied his boat tied up close to the marina office, I looked forward to a sociable get together. That was not to be however; the small group of people beginning to congregate at the office were the vanguard of a tour party. Vic was due to run them down river, then across the bay to Vancouver.

I told him, in the few minutes we had, he could release the plane. I also insisted, that if he hadn't yet prepared a bill for me—he'd better think up a number fast, as I wasn't sure how long I intended staying around. He thought fast all right—but low. A dash on the frugal side I thought; so I added a bit, and paid him.

I contemplated, as I walked back up the ramp, how Aubrey's generosity to me seemed to have warped my judgement, insofar as this sudden and uncharacteristic act on my part was concerned. Peeling off additional reimbursements, is not a thing my nature normally encourages.

Vic had been obviously pleased...I'd experienced pain when I'd said it was nothing.

CHAPTER SEVENTEEN

The sightseeing tour of Richmond, with Irene the waitress, turned out to be one of those pleasant little episodes that befall the lucky wanderer.

Richmond, is the location of the Vancouver International Airport, the Regency Hotel, and Irene's apartment. It also boasts more shopping centres than those, who were born to shop, could possibly cope with. I got to see them all.

Fortunately, between the shopping acres, lurks a park; a sports centre with an ice-rink, several indoor swimming pools, a running track; and an arts-library building.

The park was glorious, one of the finest I've ever seen. Its focal point was a huge man-made lake, complemented by hump-backed bridges; water-lilies; several islands, which looked like floating flower gardens; and a cascading waterfall. Irene took me ice-skating.

One thing led to another; in the natural enough courses of events. When we emerged from our session with The Skaters Waltz and with our appetites whetted, and my pants wetted, from constantly mopping the ice, Irene insisted we should retire to her apartment. She would do us, she promised, a home-cooked meal, and sort my pants out.

Not the greatest cook in the world, but her after dinner service left nothing to be desired. It was also extensive...it took all night.

* * * *

The next morning, Irene apologised for having to skip off to work, but the dear lass did bring me coffee in bed, and advised me to have a lay in. I drank the coffee, and took her advice. One hates to admit it, but I needed that extra nap; I can't deny that I was wilting.

With all that hospitality from Irene, it was almost noon before I returned to the hotel; where I caught up with Aubrey in the bar.

He stood me a drink, which was a novelty.

"Beginning to wonder, where you'd dashed off to," he said.

"Dashed? You left me with things to do remember? How was your baggage; everything accounted for?"

"Oh rather; jolly good to be in some decent clothes again. Tell me; did you manage to collect, the...impounding fee, for the plane?"

"No problem," I said. "Tell me; how did you make out with Nancy?"

"Thoroughly delightful day, charming company that girl; make someone a good wife. Impeccable manners, she'd be the perfect hostess. Just what you need Harry; the girl would be an asset to you. Every man needs someone like her, an anchor in this breakneck world."

"Nice of you to tell me, I'll think about it when I need anchoring." I was more interested in how he had made out with her, which he hadn't answered.

"She's keen on you, I can tell you that. Pity you're a bit slow in that direction," he went on. "Do some wooing Harry, be gracious, be debonair, tell 'em how pretty they are, that's all you have to do, have 'em swooning in no time flat."

"Where is she?"

"No idea, right now. I left her last night after dinner, at the Vancouver Hotel. Arranged to meet some of my mining people there, and took her with me. I left her in the good hands of a young chap, who I must say, was a lot quicker off the mark than you Harry. So as I say, don't drag your heels too long."

I revised my estimate of his age.

I swung the conversation round to his immediate plans. He told me he was leaving tomorrow for Edmonton. I jotted down the dates of his schedule for the rest of his stay in Canada.

I told him I thought I'd see if I could get a seat on the afternoon's flight to London.

"So soon Harry; thought you might be staying on a while. I say; not rushing off over me asking you to take the diamonds I hope. No urgency there you know."

Assuring him it was not the reason, I explained to him there were other assignments awaiting my attention in England, without saying what they were.

He said if I was set on going then, I could deliver the diamonds to Bill Rodgers to save me any unnecessary responsibility. Rodgers, incidentally was, he informed me, authorised to issue a cheque to meet my account in full.

It wasn't incidental to me.

We said our goodbyes, as we left the bar. We promised to get together as soon as possible after he returned home. Leaving it that he would give me a ring; a couple of weeks at the outside he estimated.

There was no further mention of Helen, of which I was thankful. My suspicions concerning her, were still my own. But I felt an obligation to him, to get back now, and do some checking. I couldn't be sure I was right anyway, and what Aubrey didn't know; wouldn't worry him. As I'd seen, his first concern would be that it was putting me out, by feeling I needed to hurry on his behalf. He was that sort of bloke.

Using a phone at the desk, I gave the airline a call. They had room for me on a flight leaving at three this afternoon, so I took it, which gave me less than two hours to spare.

I packed, checked out, caught the Courtesy Bus, checked in for my flight, and had almost an hour left to cool my heels at the airport. Time to grab a sandwich and sit munching it while wondering if my haste was really necessary, I mean, I didn't have to go. Not as though I had to get back to open up the office…heaven forbid. Another perk of the "finding fiddle," is if you're there you're there; if not, tough beans. On the other hand, and for some inexplicable reason, I appeared to have developed a sense of responsibility for Aubrey. Don't ask me why, could have been a knee-jerk to his generosity. Rubbish really, that was no more that I deserved. Done my bit, all obligations fulfilled…in a brilliant manner. But then, he was such a soft vulnerable old bugger—in some ways.

It was this morning, while lying in at Irene's place, where I had time to think, that this sense of responsibility grabbed me by the throat.

Thinking, of course, can be a problem provoking business. Strange really, responsibility being a cousin of ethics, which I can ignore as if it had never been invented. If it was simply a question of ethics, my conscience wouldn't have given the merest twitch.

But when responsibility rears it's flipping head, which it did in Irene's bed; of all places, my conscience reacts as though it had just swallowed a pep-pill.

The question responsibility raised was, if I felt so damned sure about the misdemeanours of Helen, Peter, and Rowland, why wasn't I doing something about it?

"Case closed," I argued. "Not my bloody business."

"You've been paid plenty," suggested responsibility.

I knew better than to argue with that. So here I sat, munching on a soggy sandwich, being led by my nose by my conscience.

Which reminded me, I hadn't phoned Chalky to let him know I was on my way…and how about a ride from the airport.

But then, my flight was due in ten minutes before eight a.m., his time, which would mean him leaving home before six. And if he happened to be working late on his locomotive, which he probably was, it wouldn't be worth his while going to bed. With a fair amount of compassion, for me, I decided not to bother him.

Having taken the time to pick up my quota of duty-free, I almost had the door of the plane slammed in my face. I'd hardly settled in my seat, it seemed, before along with a gaggle of assorted other souls, we were thundering down the runway.

I must say, being an accomplished pilot myself, I was a more relaxed passenger. I knew now of course, it was all a matter of speed...gets you up and flying in no time. I also knew, and I was living proof; you don't have to be a genius to pilot a plane. And the pilot up front was a highly trained genius to boot, with a vast array of technology at his fingertips. I imagined him, lounging back in his seat right now, having a crafty fag perhaps, and glancing through his stock portfolio, dabbing a finger on the odd button, now and again...far cry from just me and a red Ping-Pong ball.

No, I thought, if flying is absolutely necessary; this is the way to go. I settled back, savouring a Scotch and ginger-ale, Aubrey's choice of...yesterday? Was it only yesterday!

Took me a while to realise, it was only four days ago, about this time, that I'd arrived in Vancouver. So much; and in only four days, it hardly seemed possible, but there it was.

I started to re-cap, to get the events in some sort of order in my mind. But the chap in the seat on one side of me had other ideas, he was telling me he was a born again Christian. His task in life, he told me, entailed spreading the Word. I suppose I looked a likely candidate, because he lost little time in launching a crusade. Dead keen he was. Sincere enough chap, I'm sure, had my best interests at heart, good intentions, certainly polite...and a bloody nuisance.

Didn't know what to do about him; hard to be rude to a disciple. But the stuff he was drifting in my direction, floated past in a sea of intangibles. I wished he'd been flogging dirty pictures, I could handle that.

The elderly lady sitting on the other side of me partially weaned me away from him, by telling me, between his sermons, how distraught she was at having to leave her dog behind while she went on holiday. Never should have left him; if she could get off the plane now, she would. The poor little darling would pine away, be terribly unhappy, and if he got run-over she'd never forgive herself. Poor little sod, I thought, as she finished. She hadn't though. I had to hear her confession. By her own words, she was a rotten, selfish, and uncaring woman.

I offered what comfort I could, but it was nowhere near enough.

Then I had a revelation…I changed seats with the born again chap, which put him next to the confessor. She looked as though she was coping, so I got on with my re-cap.

Four days! Time had passed so fast; had flashed past like a dog going after a milkman. Days well spent, I reflected-nights too. Too bad the way the case had developed, with the added complication of Helen's carrying-ons. If she hadn't got loose-nickered with the Cooke chap; thus causing Aubrey to banish her back to the footlights? If the two of them, Rowland and Helen, hadn't got mixed up with Hepworth and tried their hand at kidnapping? If Aubrey had been kidnapped by real villains? And when I rescued him, he had not been gun-shy of publicity; I could be going home a hero, coasting along on the press I'd get…for years. Clients would have battered at my door; throwing money. With my acumen, finesse, not to mention my fox-like cunning and enterprise, the world would have been mine for the taking.

The plane story, I could have dined out on that one forever. Publicity would have stamped the seal of believability upon it. Tell it now? I could see the scene clearly…a gathering of my acquaintances. One would be saying "Harry been to dinner lately. He has told you the plane story has he?" Another would answer "Yeah, I knew Harry had a few chipped cogs, but really! Poor chap's finally stripped his gears." I could see them sniggering, tossing eye-rolling looks at each other, spinning their fingers in mocking circles at their temples…

I'd dozed off. The dog lady was giving me the elbow. Her arms were thin; her elbows had points like needles.

We were being prepared. Tables down; meal coming up. I shovelled mine down, sloshed a glass of wine after it, declined the coffee, and went back to sleep.

We were seven hours into the flight, when next I awoke. As I sipped the coffee the stewardess obligingly brought me, it occurred to me that I'd rather over-extended myself during those four days; I felt good for the sleep. It was as well that I hadn't phoned Chalky, I felt so refreshed I resolved to hot-foot it along to Weald Hall, in the hope that Helen had not as yet vacated the premises.

If she had, then I'd talk to Aubrey's man. What was his name? I remember Aubrey mentioning him…"My man…Saunders." So I'd talk to Saunders, must be the old butler chap; he'd know where I could find Helen.

From her I'd find the other two, and was I going to hammer those sods! Then I could really close the Bexley file. Have a round or two of golf with Aubrey, by which time he would be back in his world of upper-crusting, and glad to see the back of me. With which, I could put my feet back up on the mantelpiece while I waited for another client.

I went and joined the line-up for the toilets. Had a shave while I was at it; got my face wet and brushed my smile; I was fit for human consumption.

It was a lovely morning. The sun was up and about and doing its stuff, as we made our approach to the south over some of Scotland, and almost the length of England.

As we dropped lower, the patchwork of fields stretching away forever looked wonderful. Details became more sharply defined as we descended, roads with dots…the dots becoming cars; the cars acquiring colour. The final detail, just before we thumped down on the runway, the white of a rabbit's tail bobbing through the grass of Heathrow.

I went through, 'Nothing to Declare'; and got nobbled anyway. I think quite honestly, I look a picture of innocence. Customs people; appear to think differently. Perhaps they think my appearance is a front—I'm too good to be true. Whatever their reasons, they pick on me.

Surly looking blighter this one; asked me to open my bag, which I did. I stood back; he rummaged.

I suggested, pushing my flat cap to the back of my head, "If you find the Crown Jewels in there, it's a plant. I know nothing."

"I see sir," he said with zero emotion, and carried on picking over my dirty laundry. In a show of disgust he flicked his fingers fastidiously away from himself then waved me through.

I refastened the case and moved off towards the exit.

"Just a minute sir," he raised his voice officiously, after I'd taken a couple of steps. I tried not to freeze, and turned enquiringly.

He stepped towards me. "I have reason to suspect," a pause stretched longer, as our eyes locked, "the Crown Jewels, are still in the Tower." He gave me an evil smile, and wiggled his eyebrows. A performance which clearly said, 'How do you like them apples?' He said, however, "Good-morning to you, sir."

The sod, he'd had me rattled. I was wearing a crown of jewels, and they'd just got damp. The diamonds were taped under the sweat-band in my cap.

I went through the barricade, wondering which would be the most convenient mode of transportation to get me to Weald Hall.

Nothing was convenient. Underground to Charing Cross, an hourly train service from there to Tunbridge Wells; then a taxi to the Hall.

I couldn't start on that lot before I'd had some breakfast. So I picked up the morning paper and found the cafeteria. Staked a claim on a table by dumping my bag on it, and wandered along the counter making my choices. I settled for a bunch of fried stuff, with tea.

My eye caught the 'Late News' on the folded paper as I prepared to open it…then did a double take. I read. The strangled body of Lady Helen Bexley was discovered late last night in the grounds of her home near Tunbridge Wells. A police spokesman stated, No charges at this time have been laid.

I read it through again, and again, my shocked brain refusing to believe what my eyes were seeing. I felt like an actor who gets a script change; just before the curtain goes up. The light-hearted farce, suddenly switched to a drama.

My mind groped at my theory…all shot to hell. Where do we go from here Harry? My mind gave up on the groping, and hopped about like a flea on a hot stove. Aubrey, probably on his way to Edmonton—

well he'd get brought back home in a hurry. Murder! Could it be my fault, because I'd messed about and not coughed up the ransom? Police investigation! That's me in the slammer then, for smuggling. Was the murder even connected with the kidnapping? Confusion everywhere, my previously happy state of mind turned sour. The future was looking gloomy, as it concerned me.

Phone Bill Rodgers, I thought. Aubrey had given me his number. 'Do me a favour Bill', I could say, 'don't tell the police about the kidnapping'. No good, he'd have to. Come on Harry use your loaf. I did. Then I phoned Bill Rodgers.

He wasn't home, there was no answer. Try Weald Hall, probably there, I punched in the Bexley number.

"Bexley residence," a male voice answered.

"Your name Saunders,"

"It is, sir. May I inquire who is speaking?"

"Is Mr. Rodgers there?"

"He is, sir."

"Get him Saunders."

"Just one moment sir."

I heard the phone put down; then I heard the murmur of voices in the background.

The phone was picked up, "Rodgers here."

"Harry Potts." I said, and let it hang.

"Oh...where are you?"

"Heathrow, and just seen the morning paper."

"I see. Yes...a terrible business; great shock." He let that hang.

"Have you managed to contact Sir Aubrey?"

"Yes. He's on his way back now, should be arriving where you are at eleven-fifty this morning."

"All right Bill. Thank you." I rang off.

Finding a seat in the lounge, I sat and recalled what I knew about Bill Rodgers, which was not much. I'd never actually done any business with him. It must have been a year ago, or more; he'd phoned me and asked me to pay him a call. Lived in a flat in Kensington, I remembered: wasn't a hovel either. It labelled him as a client worth cultivating, although I never managed to. Something of a swinger, I recalled, but too old for it. About forty five, polished manner, much like Aubrey. Unlike Aubrey's, his polish was a pretty thin veneer.

He'd told me about this hypothetical friend (lot of prospective clients have them) who suspected an employee was stealing from him. His suspicions were not sufficient for him to go to the police, and he was looking for a chap like me to sort things out. The losses were considerable, and I shouldn't be too hasty in thinking it wouldn't be worth my while, which naturally enough put a different complexion on things. I'd agreed that, I most certainly would consider any proposition his friend made. Seemed to me, that was where we left it. He promising to contact his friend, who would no doubt be in touch. Which is usually the brush off; don't call me, I'll call you. He never did, naturally. I, as is my custom, and as I don't give free consultations; sent him a bill. A trifling sum it must have been, otherwise it would have been carved in my memory. He paid it, which would also have been engraved; if he hadn't. But, as to why he would recommend me to Lady Bexley, escaped me.

My mind dropped Bill Rodgers for more pressing, and current, affairs. I was sure I was right, when I put Helen in on the kidnapping. My theory couldn't be that far off. I'd have to put Rowland Cooke in there with her, as an accomplice. He was her lover.

Did he kill her? Could be; she was strangled, it said. Sort of thing a lover might do, given a reason. I tried to think of some half-decent motives. The only possible one that came to mind was fear of Aubrey reporting the kidnapping attempt, and Helen implicating him...pretty weak. All I achieved from that line of thinking was confusion.

I was still confused, without even the outline of a plan of what my future actions should be, when Aubrey came marching through the barrier.

CHAPTER EIGHTEEN

A subdued smile played with Aubrey's lips as he saw me and he said, "Quite a shock, eh Harry?"

"Quite a shock," I repeated, stalling to see if I could judge his state of mourning.

He appeared to sense my thoughts. "I think we can dispense with commiserations," he said. "You Harry, are one of the few people who knew the situation between Helen and myself. I'm not saying of course, that I would have wished a thing like this on her; that goes without saying. But I'm not shedding tears either, so there is no need for you to concern yourself about me. Now, how did you come to find out about this business?"

"It's in the morning paper."

"Damn...yes, I suppose it would be."

"I called Bill Rodgers," I said. "He told me you were on your way, I thought I'd wait. We need to talk; the police will want to know about the kidnapping."

He looked at me with a frown. He opened his mouth to comment, but his eyes swept to a point over my shoulder.

"Edwards," he said. "Good to see you."

I turned. His words were addressed to a chauffeur.

"Good to see you Sir Aubrey," the man in the peaked cap said. "May I say how sorry I am sir."

"Thank you Edwards"

The chauffeur turned his attention to the porter, who was following with Aubrey's luggage.

Aubrey turned his attention back to me. "Have anyone here to meet you Harry, any commitments?"

"None, except the need to talk to you."

"Good. Give your bag to Edwards then. Come back to the Hall with me; be pleased if you could actually."

"Thank you," I said.

We moved off, the porter following with my solitary bag added to his load. Edwards forged ahead. A few minutes wait at the curb-side, and a Rolls glided to rest in front of us. Aubrey and I were ushered in then the luggage was loaded.

As the car pulled away, Aubrey opened the sliding glass partition between us and the chauffeur. "Right, Edwards, let's have it. What do you know about this shocking affair?"

"Well Sir Aubrey, it was me who found her Ladyship. Ten o'clock last night it was. In the grounds just outside the library doors, I ran for Mr. Saunders, and he came back with me sir, to see for himself like. I stayed with…her, sir, while Mr. Saunders went and phoned the police. He come back after, and we both stayed there until the police arrived. Then they took over."

"I see. Do you know what she was doing out there? Had she entertained anyone last evening?"

"No sir. Her ladyship spent the evening at home, alone. I think the police think she was lured out there by whoever murdered her."

"Yes…quite. Who is at the Hall now?"

"Mr. Rodgers is there sir, taking charge, so to speak. And the police, they're all over the place."

"Hmm…Put your foot down then." Aubrey added, just before the glass partition clicked shut, "And I don't want to see anything overtake us."

Aubrey settled back in the seat, grooming his budding beard with his fingertips. He was, I would say, giving matters some thought.

As the seat and I, were programmed to be together for the next hour or so, I settled back too.

Edwards had his foot down all right. The scenery was floating past at well over a mile a minute. And nothing passed us from behind.

I had a chuckle to myself, at the view I was getting of Aubrey in his natural habitat sweeping along through life, knee deep in serfs, and issuing orders. And, I ventured, feeling responsible for the welfare of all the serfs.

I wished they could have had the opportunity to see him as I had. At first the pompous tramp, scuffing my vomit from his shoes. Then the reckless victim fighting back, creeping up on one of the villains with a club at the ready. The boyish adventurer, who egged me on to get us up in the air in the bid to escape.

"What's amusing you?"

"Showed, did it." I said. "Glad I wasn't playing poker."

"Well it showed that time. I'm sure you would be quite safe though behind a hand of cards. You don't ordinarily give much away. Pretty deep I'd say; for a young fellow. That's not to say your face is devoid of expression. But, if you'll pardon me for saying so, the expression you show is one of subdued violence. To put it another way; you look an aggressive cuss Harry. I know when you backhanded the chap Don the other morning I wasn't surprised he told us all he knew. And breaking that chap's arm in St. James'; bit drastic. So you don't only look an aggressive cuss Harry, I've no doubt you are. But then, I suppose you have to be, in your line of business. Never mind lad, your grin earns you a lot of forgiveness I'm sure. Anyway, you said you wanted to talk to me, so let's have it."

Aggressive cuss, I wasn't sure whether I'd just been given a character evaluation, or grounds for slander.

"I'll volunteer some information first," I said. "Then we'll talk. Let us go back to when I was called in on the kidnapping. You remember I told you about the two chaps in a Morris?"

He nodded, so I presumed he did.

"One of them was Rowland Cooke." I gave it to him straight.

And he took some time to react. "Really..." he eventually said. "Sets a chap to wondering, what?"

"I should hope so. You're wife is...make that was, having an affair with him, and he turns out to be one of the kidnappers. Yes, you're entitled to a wonder or two."

"That evil young swine, I'm beginning to put some thoughts together now. Cooke worked in one of my enterprises. As a diamond broker, that tells us something Harry."

"Tell me," I said, "then we'll both know."

"He'd know the diamonds to ask for; for the ransom...and he'd know how to dispose of them. So that's who was behind it all?"

"He was behind there somewhere, but I don't think he was a front-runner. There's more, answer this for me. When you confided your marital problem to me, and the outcome of it; I thought if fair to assume that Helen would hate your guts. Did she give you that impression?"

"Not an impression my boy nor in those words, but yes, I'd say you're pretty close to the mark."

"That wasn't the part she played when interviewing me for the job of messenger boy. Quite the reverse, she portrayed the loving, caring, wife. On the phone, when I called to tell her I was on my way to redeem you, she almost reduced me to tears, although, as you said, she was an actress."

I waited for him to work that out. In all fairness, it had taken me a while; and I knew more than he did.

"Are you telling me then; Helen was also involved?"

"Let's say, I'm hinting."

"You knew this then...before you left Canada. You should have told me, Harry," he said reproachfully.

"You're right, I should. However, for reasons which at that time I felt were valid, I decided not to. I thought a word in Helen's, and or

Rowland's ear, informing them I was aware of their plot, would be the
way to go. Circumstances have altered, so now I'm telling you."

"They broke the law Harry. I'll see that Cooke is charged, of
course. He'll go to prison, if he's proven guilty.

"There's the rub; on the evidence I can some up with, he won't
even be charged. That is one of the reasons I decided not to tell you
in the first place. Only one thing was certain, you would have been in
the headlines. You didn't seem keen on that."

"Hrrmm, I see, yes I do see…you really are a decent chap. It
shouldn't surprise me: you've shown me your true metal before. You
could have just walked away couldn't you? You weren't obliged to do
anything. I'm grateful, again."

I swung the conversation on a different tack. "There is one more
thing; the diamonds."

"What about them. Haven't lost them have you?"

"No. But very shortly now, we'll be telling the police about the
kidnapping, along with all the details, right?"

"Won't have any options," he said thoughtfully, "Been taken out
of our hands, hasn't it?"

"Sums it up well, only thing is; if we mention taking the diamonds
for a ride to Canada, and back; I'll be in trouble, I think."

"You and me both," he finally accepted. "Accessory after the fact,
I should think, or before, or between. I did ask you to bring them back."

"Look," I suggested. "We don't have to tell outright lies, we sort of
leave it floating in the air that the diamonds never left England.

"Could you manage that Harry? Intimate, without lying?"

"No problem!" I offered.

"Good: then you do it. I shall refer all questions concerning my
captivity to your feats of imagination. If they want to know how the
bloody shed was furnished, I'll tell 'em. Anything else…it's over to
you. Tell them what you think is best. After the tale you spun that
chap Vic, I have great confidence in you." He chuckled. "Wouldn't
mind hearing it actually; hope I'm around when you tell it. Too bad
you weren't able to shield me from publicity Harry, but thanks for
trying. I'll just have to make the best of it."

I peeled the diamonds one by one out of my cap, popping them back in their suede pouch as I did so.

He laughed as I handed the pouch to him.

I laughed too: "Make the best of it," he'd said about publicity. I certainly intended too.

CHAPTER NINETEEN

The Rolls, as it whispered through the final curve in the journey, revealed to us the imposing entrance of Weald Hall.

A gaggle of parked vehicles, outside the gates, disgorged their occupants as the Rolls eased to a stop in front of the closed gates.

A police constable posted at the gates approached the Rolls. Words were exchanged between him and our chauffeur. The gates were opened.

During the brief stop, the people from the parked cars gathered round the Rolls. Faces peered through the windows. I was pleased to see them. The press, were pressing.

I recognised one of them; Sam Jenkins, from the Daily Express. His coverage of the Finchly affair, had been my ticket to earning a living in the finding game. He recognised me too. He smiled, almost imperceptibly, and pulled his ear-lobe suggestively. I offered him a friendly wink to suggest his message had been received and understood as we rolled through the gates.

The gardeners were not in evidence as we drove along the driveway. They had been replaced by the 'boys in blue', whose interests though, appeared to be of a similar nature. They too, were bending over and paying attention to the lawns and borders.

Bill Rodgers met Aubrey, followed closely by myself in the entrance hall. Rodgers introduced us to Detective Inspector Archibald Wilson, who looked as sharp as a ferret and didn't say much. Aubrey addressed the old butler chap as Saunders. So I'd got that right.

Little of the initial conversation was tossed in my direction. I wasn't offended—I observed and listened.

Bill Rodgers, verbally adroit, skilfully made it plain to Aubrey that the police were uninformed regarding the kidnapping.

Detective Inspector Wilson contributed the bare facts of Helen's murder, which tallied with what we already knew. Person or persons unknown had strangled Lady Bexley. They had, according to Wilson, very little to go on, which was Aubrey's cue to abandon me in favour of urgent matters to be discussed with Bill Rodgers.

So D.C.Wilson; mid-fortyish; thin-faced, with extremely sharp eyes, decided he would like to talk to me. We were ushered by Saunders into the drawing room.

Sensible chap Saunders. He offered coffee, which I quickly accepted over the mild protestations of Wilson. Saunders arranged for it; served it, and generally hung around as long as he could which gave me plenty of time to formulate what I was going to dish up to the inspector. Time too, to get a cigar underway, always a good aid when the need to waffle arises.

Wilson started the ball bouncing by asking me about my status with Sir Bexley, which gave me, with a minimum of stogie fiddling, a smooth run into the kidnapping.

I offered a censored account of the happenings relating to it, diverting his interest away from what I felt might not be in my best interests, by volunteering information he could get his sharp teeth into. The names of the occupants of the Morris, for instance, he liked that. I also coughed up Peter Hepworth's comments during our meeting in St. James. Naturally I avoided the matter of the ten thousand quid…like the plague. I showed him the photographs Chalky had taken at the Palace, which diverted his attention a bit. He was pleased with them.

He called his sergeant in about that time, who got busy with a notebook.

They both seemed quite pleased with me; when I was able to provide them with the number of the Morris, along with a detailed description of Peter Hepworth, and a good enough one of Rowland Cooke. I thought I was going to get a round of applause.

My presence after that though, lost star billing. But I managed to rise in the ratings when I proffered information concerning the Bexley's estrangement. Cooke's leading role in that affair really grabbed them.

Earned me a reprieve; Aubrey suddenly became a much more desirable person to question than I did. But as I said to Wilson; although I failed to see how it could possibly relate to Lady Bexley's demise, he, as a professional might well read something in it. He liked the last bit too, and became quite matey towards me.

I did manage a few words with Aubrey, before he took over my spot in the limelight. He invited me to come back later, suggesting I come for dinner then spend the evening with him and Bill Rodgers; I accepted

Chauffeur Edwards was then summoned to drive me home. I thought they could have invited me to lunch before I left, but my growling stomach apparently went unnoticed.

Sam Jenkins of the Express was still in attendance at the gate as I was driven out. I gave him a wave, which I felt would give him enough encouragement to phone me.

Edwards handed me my bag, after he'd let me out in front of my cottage. Nice enough chap Edwards; we'd had a good natter on the way home. I've found it never hurts to probe the hired help, all sorts of peripheral tit-bits can be gathered that way. I didn't reap many from him, but one has to try. I made a few discreet enquiries regarding Grace Watkins. She was, it seemed, in good health. Full of remorse I expect, about missing having her way with me. I also thought I'd give her another chance.

Mrs. H came trotting through the front door to meet me. "I'm glad you've come, Mr. Potts," she panted, "The phone's been having fits." Which roughly translated, meant it had been ringing frequently. Mrs. H. has those at times, usually when she gets agitated.

"How are you Mr. Potts?" she asked, scurrying ahead of me through the door.

"Hungry," I informed her. She zoomed off like a heat-seeking device, homing in on the kitchen stove.

The phone rang before I'd had time to put my bag down. It was Sam Jenkins.

I took the time to whet his appetite, telling him he was onto a very good thing. Behind the murder lurked a kidnapping, involving a ransom in diamonds and high adventure in the shape of a hair-raising escape in a borrowed float plane. I gave him, as a sample; the names of Hepworth and Cooke, who the police would be looking for to help with their enquiries. I promised him an exclusive. Not yet…but stay tuned.

When I got rid of him, I called Chalky. He wanted to know when I was coming home, because the case had taken a nasty turn. When I stole his thunder, by telling him I knew about the murder, because I was already home, he got cranky. What the hell, why was I home without calling him to meet me? What the hell had I been up to? He hoped I realised that there was a good chance my 'arsing about' had been the cause of the murder? When could we get together?

I told him I had been chauffeured home in the Bexley Rolls. I chose to ignore his other questions, except the last. To that one, I told him my schedule was tight right now, being as I was in great demand at Weald Hall, to help the police with their enquiries.

That drew from him, "I'll bloody well bet you are!"

Unruffled, I explained that although I wasn't sure when I would be free; I would make every effort to see him on the morrow.

To which, he answered, "Tomorrow? You'll be lucky, if you're still free to walk the sodding streets." He rang off.

By this time, Mrs. H had produced a Welsh Rarebit and ordered me to sit at the table and eat it.

I ate to the accompaniment of a narrative by Mrs. H on the happenings during my absence. Nothing had looked any different to me as the Rolls came through the village. So much for my powers of observation! The hamlet as a whole, according to Mrs. H's, disclosures, was a seething cauldron of intrigue and infidelity. I was flabbergasted at the things that had gone on under those roofs. And all in four days!

With the Welsh Rarebit a memory, with strawberries and cream but a lingering taste, the revelations continued, she'd used up the four days, but moved right along into the future. A visit to a fortune-teller, and there was certainly some cracking stuff in the cards for Mrs. H.

I set fire to a cigar and listened, spellbound. All to do with the initials of people who were due to cross her path. She'd been given the low-down on those to watch out for. None of the initials fitted me. What self-respecting soothe-sayer would come up with H P? Her clients would think she was reading it off the sauce bottle. I found the courage about that time, to do a bunk. I was decent enough to make my break during a slight pause between topics.

Whipping upstairs, I hurriedly unpacked, threw most of the contents in the laundry basket then nipped out to the comparative isolation of the bike shed. I lifted the covers from the bikes, looked them over, dusting them with a rag as I did so. Then drifted over to the garage, started the Bentley up, and backed her out for an airing. The old girl looked as though a wash wouldn't do her any harm. I was mentally rolling up my sleeves to get started, when Mrs. H came bustling out.

"The phone again Mr. Potts, Sir Aubrey Bexley, no less, and he's holding. So you had better not keep him waiting." She made it sound like a royal command.

She's keen on royals and titles, is Mrs. H. I'd have been a disappointment to her, had I not made a show of deference by getting a move on.

Now, what the hell does he want, I wondered? I had said I would see him this evening...so what's urgent? Probably wants to remind me to dress for dinner. What does he think I am; some kind of peasant.

"Here," I said, as I picked up the phone.

"Yes Harry, more news. Inspector Wilson has just informed me that Rowland Cooke has been found."

"That was fast," I said, wondering about his use of the word found.

"Not fast enough. He's dead; apparently committed suicide. His body was fished out of the Thames this morning. His car was located, it had been abandoned close by. Wilson now thinks Cooke murdered Helen for some reason then threw himself in the river, in a fit of remorse."

"Well, that keeps it all nice and tidy," I suggested.

Wilson thinks so, yes. They'll poke around, he says: see if they can find anything conclusive. But he thinks it just about puts the lid on things. I've invited him to join us tonight for dinner, so no doubt we'll hear more then. Thought I'd let you know Harry, and we'll see you for dinner tonight then?"

"Right," I confirmed.

I walked back to the Bentley, forgot about washing her; and sat on the running board, for a think.

I put myself in his shoes…Cooke's, their shoes; mustn't forget Hepworth. What sort of reaction would the escape of Aubrey and myself, have prompted? I should think they would expect to be in the mire over the kidnapping. They couldn't hope that Aubrey wouldn't report the matter to the police, after the event. Which he would have I'm sure even if Helen hadn't been murdered. For one of them to have murdered her, didn't make too much sense; be like sending the police an invitation to investigate them. What about Hepworth, he seemed to have got on the back burner. Was he shutting mouths? Easy to push Cooke in the river, and make it look like a suicide, not very likely that I could put the finger on him. But then, I could be on his hit list too! Nah, I'd eat him, and unless he was a slow learner he'd know it

Suppose though, there was a fourth party involved, someone with a lot to lose, someone who could be implicated by Helen, Cooke, or Hepworth. Well now, two down—and one to go.

Who gained most by the kidnapping? Well, Aubrey gained, if Helen's murder was connected to the kidnapping. He got rid of a wife he wanted to get rid of. And that, I should think, could easily top the list of motives for murder. But then, Aubrey didn't have to kill Helen, he already had the evidence to divorce her.

What about the little item which had come out in the confession by Don? The English big shot, who arranged his own kidnapping? All they had to do, he'd said, was make it look real: looked real enough to me! Although: Aubrey had gone a shade red in the face, when I asked him if he'd been up to some hanky-panky. Aubrey?

What about the taped message I'd received over the phone? From Aubrey, saying he was in good health, and to cough up the ransom— or words to that effect.

He had never once mentioned that message to me. But he had said that during his incarceration, as he put it; he had seen no one, or heard a man made sound. So how did he make the recording?

And what a great alibi to have when your wife gets murdered, "Well, I was being held hostage at the time, don't you know." he would say. But he wasn't, he'd been released by the time she was killed. He was still in Canada though.

Harry, you have slipped a cog. Aubrey and a crew of accomplices to boot, give me a break!

My brain was in danger of giving itself a rupture, so I took the strain off it. I got up, walked back into the cottage, and found the tape cassette containing Aubrey's message. Returning to the Bentley, with it and the recorder, I sat down on the running board again.

I put the recorder and the cassette together, and pressed the play button.

The recording began: 'Harry Potts?' my acknowledgement followed. 'Got a message for you', a pause, then Aubrey came on. 'This is Sir Aubrey Bexley speaking. I am advising you of my good health. I confirm that a newspaper being shown to me is dated July the twenty-second. Please comply with monetary arrangements as suggested'.

I switched the recorder off...I was dumbfounded. The two timing sod: Harry the clot. But I was on to the bastard now. I felt my ire rising, I could almost feel my hands on his throat. I'd shake the devious bugger 'til his balls rattled'.

CHAPTER TWENTY

The constable was still on duty as I rolled the Bentley up to the gates of the Hall. I gave him my name, and he opened them for me.

Aubrey was smoothly courteous when Saunders ushered me in to join him, Bill Rodgers, and Detective Inspector Wilson.

Aubrey was also the perfect host during pre-dinner drinks, and throughout the excellent meal that followed.

Wilson, as Aubrey had forecast, briefly summarised his investigation.

In his view: Lady Bexley and Cooke and Hepworth had conspired together in the execution of the kidnapping. The murder of Lady Bexley and also the apparent suicide of Cooke were almost without doubt connected. The obvious link, of course being Hepworth, who, Wilson revealed, had a criminal record—for crimes of violence.

Wilson professed his confidence in Hepworth's imminent arrest and his being charged shortly thereafter with the murder of Lady Bexley.

Wilson was not however, quite as confident, when it came to charges being laid in connection with the kidnapping.

At this point I asked. "Can we take it then Inspector, that if the evidence won't substantiate charges, the kidnapping can be kept under wraps?"

He shook his head. "No chance of that. The media already have their noses into it, and it's my guess they'll make a circus out of it."

The conversation then drifted to sundry other matters as we approached the end of the meal.

Idle chatter really. Aubrey and Bill Rodgers were both keen snooker players it appeared. So with dinner over, Aubrey suggested we should retire to the billiard room and pot a few balls.

Aubrey and Bill offered to partner Wilson and myself, but the Inspector declined the invitation; saying he wasn't a very good player, but he enjoyed watching.

Aubrey, as host, broke. He had the longest cue anyway.

His cue ball struck the reds just right. Two red balls rolled clear, one found the pocket, the other teed itself up. The cue ball came back into balk. Aubrey was going to be tough to beat.

He looked up at me, giving me one of his self-satisfied smirks. I decided it was time to take the smirk off his face.

"I've wondered," I said, making a production of chalking my cue. "Why you didn't ever mention, the message you taped concerning your well-being?"

"Eh, what message is that? What the devil are you talking about Harry?"

"I'm talking about you and the kidnapping. I'm sure you remember someone telling me a story of the English big shot who arranged his own kidnapping. I played that tape back again today...it revealed a lot to me."

His mouth tightened; I'd taken the smirk off it. "I told you that was a lot of rubbish."

I produced the tape from my inside jacket pocket, and held it up. "Do you have a player?"

He pointed to the corner of the billiard room. I walked over and inserted the tape in the hi-fi system, and touched the play-button.

I rejoined the group at the table as the tape began.

"This is Sir Aubrey Bexley speaking…"

I watched Aubrey's face as the tape revealed its contents. His expression displayed bewilderment, quickly changing to suppressed anger; then stunned shock.

His eyes broke away from mine, and turned to Bill Rodgers. "You bastard! That's your voice!"

I watched Bill Rodgers face. The blood drained from his features. His eyes looked away from Aubrey, darting from mine to Wilson's.

He looked like he was regaining his composure. I knew he was a smooth talker…given thinking time.

He wasn't going to get it, reversing the cue I'd picked up. I smashed it across Rodgers' shins. A vicious blow, I got both of them; a double crack.

Judging by the shriek of pain that escaped his clenched teeth, I felt his thinking time had been terminated.

In case it hadn't, I pulled the cue back for another swipe at the sod. He dropped to his knees; his reflexes were still working…his shins were denied me.

"You filthy conniving bugger," I snarled, with the stick poised at the top of the backswing. "You've got about two seconds to start talking."

I looked him over for another high-pain area, and chose his head. "I'll brain you," I muttered, as I lined up on my new target. I'd made my commitment, I was getting desperate. With nothing forthcoming from him…I was going to look pretty stupid. The thought put plenty of determination in my face as I started to swing…

"No. For God's sake," he screamed. "No more."

His eyes looked up pathetically at Aubrey. "He's right. I did it for Helen. I wanted you dead. And then God help me—I had to kill her." His voice broke. Tears streamed down his face. He leaned forward, covered his face with his hands, and sobbed.

With a sigh of relief, I put the stick down and looked across at Aubrey. His countenance showed absolute disgust.

"Get up, you swine," he snapped at Rodgers. "At least try to act like a man." He turned to Wilson. "Take his statement Inspector, or whatever it is you do now. Then remove this...article from my home." With which, he squared his shoulders, and marched out of the room.

Inspector Wilson stood shaking his head; I thought he was probably bewildered. But he turned to me saying, "I never witnessed him accidentally tripping over your billiard cue! Send for the Constable on the gate; tell him to get in here, and you...stay out of the room. I'll talk to you later."

I left the room. I sent the message to the constable. I caught up with Aubrey in the hallway. We were still standing saying nothing, when Saunders came through with the constable in tow.

As Saunders drew abreast, Aubrey broke the silence. "Scotch, Saunders, in the library, and don't hang about."

In the library, Aubrey threw himself into an armchair with something between a sigh and a growl. With a flap of his arm he waved me into another armchair facing him.

"All right Harry, tell me. Bare facts will do."

So I did, the bones of the matter, as I saw them.

"Let's go back to the beginning," I began.

"You mentioned your wife being guilty of several indiscretions. We now know Rodgers was one of them. He wanted you dead, he said. So we also know why we were never meant to leave the lake alive. I think Rodgers had been waiting for an opportunity to dispose of you, without risk to himself, naturally. With you out of the way, all sorts of bonus points popped up for him. Presumably Helen would inherit from you...he would marry Helen. So then, with you dead he'd get your wife, and your wealth.

"To get on...this Canadian trip comes up. He'd know well in advance, right; here's the opportunity, he thinks, so he cooks up an idea for a kidnapping. It gives him a bit on the side for his honeymoon expenses...a bag of diamonds. He'd need accomplices in Canada of course and one in England...a front man.

"I'm sure Rodgers had some kind of hold over Cooke. He once told me a hypothetical story about an employee who was a little on the light-fingered side, that employee could have been Cooke.

"Whatever; Rodgers pulls Cooke into the office one day, and runs this past him. For reasons, which Cooke need not concern him self with, Sir Aubrey wanted to stage a bogus kidnapping, with himself as the victim. Cooke would be required to perform certain duties to assist in this endeavour. If he carried them off satisfactorily, Cooke could get back to knocking off the odd gem again. Put like that, Cooke would naturally say, 'Just tell me what!'

Rodgers tells him: set up the snatch in Canada; tell the lads over there not to worry, it isn't for real.

"Oh yes, and here in England, Cooke is to get someone to hold up the messenger and relieve him of the ransom. The messenger would have to believe it was a genuine kidnap, because he would be the one the police would question, should they be called in.

"Cooke happens to know just the chap for the hold-up, a friend of his Hepworth, a villain with a criminal record who was always ready to earn a few extra bob.

"Bit of luck here, because Hepworth has some contacts in Canada. Hank the pilot, and his brother Don. Hank gets told the tale about it being a set-up. "Not to worry" says Hepworth. 'It's this English big-shot, who wants to make out like he's being kidnapped, but make it look real'. Hank would hardly raise an eyebrow; the guy being English…all odd-balls.

"So, give or take a bit that was the plan. Rodgers tells Helen, who after you giving her the old heave-ho becomes a very willing accomplice, to give me a call. He had me down on his not-too-bright list. I wasn't too bright because I hadn't read the script, so I went and buggered things up for them…I wouldn't give them the diamonds.

"Then when Hepworth reported back, via Cooke, that I won't play until I get a message from you, Rodgers makes the tape. He knew I wouldn't know your voice. He probably guessed I might play it back to Helen, so she gets tipped off to expect it. Then, with appropriate sobs from her, she sends me off to the rescue.

"Moving along a bit, when Rodgers gets your call from Canada, he panics, which would be putting it mildly. He knows you'll take me with you, and report the whole mess to the police. But we don't know who the guilty parties are, he thinks; except I know now who the two blokes in the Morris were. One of them, Cooke, knows Rodgers is involved. And so does Helen. Two people then…who have to be silenced.

"He phones Helen last night, saying he has to talk to her. Possibly they had kept their distance, while the plot was going on, so he tells her they'd better meet secretly…in the garden, outside these doors…where he strangles her.

"Then off he goes, and phones Cooke. Tells Cooke to meet him…wherever Cooke's car was found abandoned, conks him on the noggin and slings him in the river. And those, Aubrey," I concluded," and as you asked…are the bare facts."

"Glad I didn't ask for details," said Aubrey, twitching his eyebrows while pouring his third scotch. "This chap Hepworth then, must be wetting has pants, if he knows about Helen and Cooke. He'll think he's next on the list, won't he?"

"Every chance," I said. "I know, if I was in his shoes…the thought would cross my mind.

"The thing is though, if he doesn't know about Rodgers' involvement; he'll think it's you Aubrey, who is nipping round closing mouths."

Aubrey sat shaking his head. "What the devil is the world coming to Harry, I'm beginning to lose track of what's what. Those bare facts, you've just spouted, were not one of your cock-and-bull stories were they?"

"Partly, I suppose," I conceded. "Bet I'm not far wrong though."

"Hmm,. But how much" he queried, "do you actually know?"

"Actually, about as much as you do. You heard the tape, and what Rodgers said."

"And that was enough, all you had to go on, to do what you did in the billiard room?"

"Enough for me" I said. "I played the tape this afternoon, and recognised Rodgers' voice. Coming here tonight, and knowing you, Rodgers, and the Inspector would be together. I figured it was one of those 'now-or-never' situations. If I had any chance of getting to the bottom of things, I had to get maximum mileage from the tape. I also needed you there when it was played...you would know it was Rodgers' voice. The Inspector was a must too. But most of all, I needed Rodgers in a relaxed frame of mind; I had to shock him. I was sure he thought he was in the clear, and if you've got a bomb to drop, that's the time to do it. The tape rattled him all right. But not quite enough, so I went for his shins.

Aubrey, swilling the scotch in his glass, smiled. "Tell me Harry, what would you have hit him with, if we hadn't moved to the billiard room?"

I thought about that a while, then grinned back at him, "One of the candelabra, I expect."

He laughed; a sound I was happy to hear. I realised I'd grown quite fond of the silly bugger.

But before I got maudlin, I said. "Been an interesting evening Aubrey, and I hate to eat and run, but I'm going to."

"Run? What are you dashing off for...I mean to say...the Inspector...your statement...don't you want to hear what Rodgers has confessed to?"

"Absolutely," I agreed. "Perhaps you will be good enough to tell the Inspector I'll look in on him tomorrow. Something came up you see, that's why I have to scoot."

"Hrrmm, bit much Harry. Felt sure you'd be staying on for a while, and all that." He tossed his hands about to indicate the scope of...all that.

"Sorry, can't be done," I said, standing up.

Fact of the matter was, when Saunders was serving me coffee earlier today he had handed me a note.

"From Miss Grace," he'd said.

Harry Darling, the note read, I've missed you. I'm ready to get to know you. I hope you'll come tonight; however late.

It sounded to me, like things were loosening up.

"Good-night Aubrey," I said.